# THE POWERS OF KING GATESKIN

Gateskin Chronicles Book 5

JANICE SPINA

PUBLISHED BY JANICE SPINA


Londonderry, New Hampshire

COVER BY JOHN SPINA



ISBN (paperback) 979-8-9874646-8-7

Library of Congress Control Number: 2026903844

# CHARACTERS IN BOOK 5 - The Powers of King Gateskin

Spindle - Head Guard

Mitteran - 2nd Head Guard in command (previously from Parotovina as HG)

King Gateskin -King Wizard of Sovorotskina

Queen Solinara -Queen Fairy of Sovorotskina

Serena - eldest daughter of KG & QS - 16 yrs old - can fly, move objects with her mind and read minds, talk to animals

Simon - son of KG & QS - 14 years old - can fly and talk to animals

Catalina - daughter of KG & QS - 12 years old - can blend into surroundings and become invisible

Hotenfaran - brother of Solinara

Procelina - wife of Hotenfaran

Jennara & Henno - powerful couple, immigrants from Parotovina

Abason & Anabal - parents of Spindle

Botular - former spy of King Kaposkaran of Parotovina now residing in Sovorotskina - still causing trouble

Aharona - dragon lady from Dragonaria

Callum - Aharona's dragon - multi-colored, rainbow body, sweeter than Evander with green eyes

Navaeha – sister of Aharona from Dragonaria

Evander – Navaeha's dragon – larger wings, blue, red and gold scales with blue eyes fierce to others but adores Navaeha

Elowen – oldest sister of Aharona and Navaeha uses Dark Magic

Jelitza – cousin of Aharona, Navaeha & Elowen

Verite – Jelitza's dragon – a sweet female, strong and resilient, silver scales and eyes

Mianna – former foe now friend of Aharona and Navaeha

Marcellus & Isla – parents of dragon ladies of Dragonaria King & Queen of Dragonaria

Wolves - Cantok leader

Notak - Cantok's mate

King Cavelan - King of Votovia

Queen Savina - Queen of Votovia

King Kaposkaran - King of Parotovina

Quintal - first Quintaroon

Taron - second Quintaroon

Madrigal - male dragon to go to live with KG for 2 weeks on trial basis (turquoise dragon) turquoise eyes

Izara - Madrigal's mate who will live with KG on 2 weeks trial basis (purple dragon) purple eyes

Sunniva - sun gift - female dragonet - yellow & turquoise scales

Lorcan - fierce - male dragonet - red & purple scales

Silas - old villager of Sovorotskina

Marion - villager of Sovorotskina - strong-willed and outspoken

Wizards:

Head Wizard - Marno

Wizard #2 - Fortag

Wizard #3 - Wassor

Wizard #4 - Tornak

Catlings - catlike creatures live in UT

Rabbinels - creatures created by Queen Solinara and Hotenfaran to feed the wolves and fulfill the need of the wolves to hunt and forage for food

Quintaroon's Powers:

1. Can fly
2. Formidable size and strength
3. Dangerous claws and jaws
4. Can become invisible if it drinks water
5. Can shrink or grow in size if it eats people

Weaknesses:

1. Afraid of the dark
2. Blinded by bright light
3. Fears rodents like squirrels, mice and rats

4. **Allergic to nuts**

**SPELLS:**

**Transformation spell (used to assist Quintaroons in returning to human state**

**Sprite's Spell (used to bring shrunken Sprite back to his former size after beam of light shrunk him)**

**Exaggeration of the Truth Spell (EOT) (used on Parotovinan Guards who came to cause havoc in Sovorotskina to send them home without any memory of what transpired in Sov)**

**Lock Spell (used to lock Quintaroons in their house)**

Moss Spell - to rid the land of growing moss - puts animals to sleep (for Catlings)

Farm Animals of Gateskin:

Hank the horse

Milly the cow

Chickens & pigs

EVIL ONES - EOs

TAKEN ONES - TOs

DESCENDANTS OF TOs - DOTO

# VILLAGES/RULERS:

Sovorotskina – Land of Goodness & Light – King Gateskin/Queen Solinara

Parotovina – Land of Evil & Darkness - -King Kaposkaran/Queen Beregina

Votovia – Land of Magic & Mystery -- King Cavelan/Queen Savina

Amora – Land of Faith & Love – King Noderan/Queen Davora

Merona – Land of Peace & Harmony – Ruled by Healers

Merlina – Land of Myths & Legends – King Zuri/Queen Zuleima

## PLACES/RIVERS/FORESTS:

Crotesia - Mountain, cave at base where EO took Gateskin (borders Amora, Merlina & Parotovina)

| | |
|---|---|
| Corian Falls - | in Sovorotskina |
| Lake Serena - | In Sovorotskina (named after Gateskin's daughter, Serena) |
| Gateskin River - | in Sovorotskina and travels through Merona & Amora |
| Zaylany River - | in Merlina and |

Parotovina

Skina Forest – in Sovorotskina

Merona Forest – in Merona

Sea of Shakelle – off coast of Parotovina

Unknown Territory – territory outside of Sovorotskina – UT

Mt. Ailylene – in Sovorotskina

Mt. Sonovan – in Votovia

Mt. Amora – in Amora

Mt. Merlin – in Merlina

Mt. Harmony – in Merona

Dragonaria – Land of the Dragons

# Table of Contents

# NOELLA PROVINCE

# CHAPTER ONE

Spindle, a tree Sprite, who was King Gateskin's Head Guard, sadly gazed down on the carnage. He messaged King Gateskin, and then called out to the two dragons to come quickly. He needed them to keep the Catlings, large cat-like creatures, at bay in order to rescue the Parotovinan guards who were stranded in the UT, the Unknown Territory.

Madrigal, a male dragon, heard Spindle's cry for help and woke his mate, Izara. "We need to find out what Spindle needs."

As they were flying out of their lair, King Gateskin met them and explained what was happening.

"Why does this Parotovinan king keep sending his men here to get slaughtered?" Madrigal asked as he flew above the UT and looked down.

"I think I am going to be sick, Madrigal! I need to go back to our lair," Izara called out in alarm, her face getting paler by the second.

"What's wrong, Izara?" Madrigal flew by her side and gazed at her face.

"I don't know. But I felt sick all of a sudden after looking at that massacre below."

King Gateskin nodded to Madrigal. "Let her go back to the lair to rest. It is quite horrifying to look at. I don't blame her for feeling that way. I don't particularly feel well either."

Madrigal flew back to the lair to make sure Izara was settled before returning to assist the King and Spindle with the mess in the UT.

While Madrigal chased the Catlings away, Spindle hovered over the Parotovinan guards and plucked one or two at a time out of the UT with the help of his fellow Sprites, much to the relief of the frightened men.

"Thank you so much, Sprites," the Parotovinan men exclaimed in unison as they fell to their knees on the safe ground of Sovorotskina.

King Gateskin looked at them and waited until the men could calm down before asking, "Why are you here now? What does your king want you to do this time?"

The men exchanged looks and shook their heads. One man in charge said, "We don't want to talk about it. It is hopeless what he expects of us!"

"What did you do to the Catlings to change them like that? Did you give them a potion again?" Gateskin queried.

"We didn't know that this would happen to them. We were told to use it on the dragons. It was supposed to put them to sleep so we could get them onto the carts and bring them back to Parotovina."

"Why did you tell him that?" the Parotovinan guard in charge asked, with a stern face at his fellow guard.

"Hmm, I figured as much. But this potion you used, was it made by Queen Beregina?" King Gateskin asked.

"Umm, well, I guess it was," the guard in charge admitted.

"Now you will return home and never come back here again. Do you hear me?" Gateskin commanded the men.

"Of course, King Gateskin. We will leave immediately and never return." The Parotovinan guard looked at his men and pointed the way to return home.

The men hung their heads and moved as quickly as they could in case the King changed his mind about allowing them to go.

The King watched the guards walk away until he could not see them anymore, assuring that they were not returning.

Gateskin instructed Madrigal to incinerate the Catlings who were multiplying in hideous forms, now below. He couldn't believe his eyes how fast they were growing and separating into new Catlings. They did not look like anything he had ever seen before. Their jaws and teeth were larger and their heads appeared to grow faster than their bodies. Their legs were increasing in numbers, too, making their bodies look stranger than ever as they tried to run away.

"I will do my best to get them all, King." Madrigal blew out smoke rings to stop the deformed creatures from getting away by putting them to sleep. He next burned them with blasts of fire until they were just ashes.

Madrigal flew over all of the UT and searched for any Catlings that may have escaped. The Sprites in the trees helped him find a few more that he had missed.

Madrigal waved his wings in appreciation to the Sprites and winked at them which delighted the little tree creatures so much that they began to sing.

**We do our best to help the King**

**And aid the dragons with their magnificent wings.**

**We are friends to all if they are kind**

**And will always keep those who assist us in mind.**

Madrigal laughed out loud and waved goodbye to them in the treetops as he flew back to the lair to check on his mate.

King Gateskin thanked the Sprites for helping and sprinkled some goodies that he conjured out of thin air down to their huts in the trees much to their surprise. The Sprites called out to the King their gratitude and cheered him until he flew away.

Gateskin followed behind Madrigal to thank him and see how Izara was doing.

When he arrived back at the lair, with his powers Gateskin created two furry creatures for the dragons to enjoy.

Izara looked up but did not take the creature. She looked sickly with her pale face that was a few shades lighter than her usual purple color.

Madrigal ate the two creatures so they would not go to waste and settled down next to his mate to try to make her feel better. He wore a frown of concern as he looked up at the King.

Gateskin suggested, "I can have Solinara, my queen, come and take a look at Izara. I'm sure she will have something that will make her feel better."

"Thank you, King. I think that would be most helpful. I am worried about her. She has never been sick before like this," Madrigal expressed with a deep sigh.

King Gateskin returned home to find his wife busy in her workshop creating more food for the wolves and dragons to keep them all sated. She had also created more Rabbinels for the wolves who needed the exercise to hunt the creatures.

"I can see there is something bothering you, Gateskin," Solinara replied, when she saw the concern etched on his face.

"I think we may have a problem, Solinara."

"A problem? What kind of problem?"

He explained about the carnage in the UT and the guards that King Kaposkaran had sent once again.

"Well, it appears that Izara is sick. I asked the dragons to assist me with cleaning up the mess in the UT caused by the potion created by Queen Beregina. Izara couldn't even look down upon it without feeling sick. She had to return to the lair."

"Hmm, I see."

"What do you see, Solinara?" Gateskin watched his wife's face as she grinned and winked at him.

"What does that wink mean, and why are you grinning like a happy cat who caught the mouse?"

"I remember the days when I felt like Izara."

"Huh? What? What does that mean?"

"I will check her over and let you know shortly after I finish with this batch of food."

Gateskin shook his head. "I hope it is nothing serious, Solinara."

After a short time, Solinara said, "Okay, I am ready to see her. Are you coming, Gateskin?"

"Yes, I…of course. I am right behind you."

Solinara giggled as they flew side by side to the dragon's lair.

Gateskin looked at his wife and again shook his head and sighed. He was confused and a little perturbed by his wife's odd behavior.

When they arrived at the dragons' lair, they saw Madrigal hovering around his sick mate.

"Oh, I am so happy to see you, Queen Solinara. I have been quite worried about Izara. Can you give her something to make her feel better?"

"Of course. Let me examine her first and I will let you know what the problem is."

Madrigal nodded and moved aside. Gateskin guided the dragon out of the way and told him, "Let's go outside and give the Queen some time to make an assessment. She will share her concerns with us shortly."

"Okay. I hope she is not too sick. She has never been like this before. She always perked up quickly if she had a stomach ache. You have provided such wonderful food that has been good for us. I no longer feel hungry every minute of the day. It fills me up and a little out as you can see." Madrigal patted his belly and smiled at the King.

"Yes, I can see you are well fed and taken care of. I am happy that we have pleased you that way. I was worried that we wouldn't be able to give you enough food to keep you sated. The special food that the Queen makes for you must be working."

"No worries there, King. I am just worried about Izara. What could be causing her stomach distress?"

Before Gateskin could respond, Solinara came out of the lair with Izara close behind.

# CHAPTER TWO

"Is she all right, Queen?" Madrigal asked with a furrowed brow.

"Well, I must say that she is very well indeed, Madrigal. I think she should tell you herself," Queen Solinara grinned as she stepped aside and stood by her husband who was quite perplexed.

Gateskin leaned closer to Solinara and whispered, “What’s wrong?”

“Shh, wait a minute and you will know.”

Gateskin watched the two dragons as they discussed the situation. He observed Madrigal’s face as he suddenly was beaming and flying around in a circle above the lair.

“What is going on here?” the King asked.

Madrigal flew down and hugged his mate and stroked her back in a loving way. He smiled as much as a dragon can smile and showed his teeth to the King and Queen.

“Well, are you going to share this excitement with me?” Gateskin queried.

“Of course, my king. I had no idea that this is what was bothering Izara. I am at a loss of words right now.”

"Really? I am still waiting to hear what this is all about?" Gateskin stated in a disgruntled manner. "I hope that you will have some words to share with me."

"I'm so sorry, King. I have good news. I am going to be a father or should I say that Izara and I are going to be parents!"

"What? Are you kidding me?" Gateskin shouted in disbelief.

"Yes, that is correct, my dear," Solinara said with a grin. "It appears that she is due anytime now and there will be two because she is carrying two eggs."

"I…I…what?" the King exclaimed as he jumped up and down and ran over to congratulate the dragons.

"Isn't it unbelievable?" Madrigal stated as he couldn't stop beaming.

Gateskin reacted, "I don't know what to say? How did this happen? I mean, when did this happen, or never mind. It is too wonderful to imagine that this would happen now after you arrived here. It could have happened before at any time."

"Does this mean that we have to return to Dragonaria? Once the King finds out about this, he may request that we give up our eggs," Izara cried out in horror.

"No, you belong here, all of you. He cannot go back on his promise to give both of you to us. All will be fine. I will make sure of that, Izara. Don't worry. Just concentrate on delivering your eggs safely and watch over them until they hatch."

"Of course, King. Thank you. I plan to do just that and never leave their side," Izara sighed in relief.

Madrigal guided his mate back to her bed in their lair so that she could rest up until delivery. He planned on never leaving her side until then either.

"I think we should go home, Gateskin, and leave them alone. Madrigal will alert me when

Izara lays her eggs. There shouldn't be any problems."

"Okay, I guess so. As long as we are not needed here to do anything else," Gateskin sighed, as he looked toward the lair.

"You are too funny, dear. It's almost as if *you* were going to be a father again," Solinara giggled.

"Well, I almost feel like it. Can you imagine, Solinara, we are going to have four dragons now?"

"Yes, we are. We need to figure out how to take care of four. We will need more food and a way to keep these little dragons from getting into too much mischief once they hatch."

"Yes, I was just thinking about that too, dear. I think we need to come up with a plan to keep them contained until we can train them as we did their parents. It won't be easy since they will be like little children and have a short attention span."

"I know you will come up with a plan, Gateskin. I will be working on some new food for the little ones that will help them grow strong and resilient to any sickness."

"Good, I will have to think about this. I need to call Spindle and the Wizards for their counsel."

Solinara followed her husband to their home as she giggled over this news. It was too shocking to believe. She would have a lot of work ahead of her too. She couldn't wait to share the news with the children. They would be thrilled.

Gateskin knew that there would be problems ahead once this news spread to Noella Province and eventually to Dragonaria. He would not share these concerns with his wife. He did not want to worry her unnecessarily. He was hoping that all would go well and then he wouldn't have to worry about it anymore.

He sighed heavily and returned to the present things that he had to handle in the meantime.

# CHAPTER THREE

"I can't believe it! Are you certain, Mother?" Serena, eldest daughter of the King and Queen, queried in excitement.

"Yes, sweetheart. This is the truth. Izara will be delivering two eggs."

“Wow! This is fantastic! We will have two more dragons to ride and play with!” Catalina, youngest daughter of the King and Queen, exclaimed as she bounced around the room.

“I can’t wait to see them! How big will they be when they hatch?” Simon, son of the King and Queen asked, his eyes wide in delight.

“I imagine they will be smaller than their parents, of course, but quite large just the same. You three will have to be careful around them. They will be like mischievous children and will bite you and maybe even try to eat you.”

“Eat us?” Catalina asked in alarm.

“Yes, they will be quite hungry when they arrive and will have to be fed by their mother and me carefully.”

“But what if they try to eat you, Mother?”

“I will have Madrigal and Izara to protect me and keep them in tow.”

“What can we do to help?” Simon asked.

"Well, I will let you know when the time comes. Okay?"

"Okay, I guess. I can't wait to see what the villagers will say about this. They are anxious to meet the two dragons. Now they will meet four," Simon responded.

"That is up to your father to announce the arrival of these two new creatures to our village. Don't say a word to anyone about this just yet. We don't want to cause alarm. Also, we are trying to keep this quiet so that Dragonaria does not try to take them away from us."

"Can they do that, Mother? Will they do that?" Serena questioned in shock.

"We don't know what they will do. That is up to your father again to handle this situation. He believes that the dragons are our property now no matter what."

"I hope so, Mother. I am worried about losing them. They will be our pets and we need to take care of them. No one should take them from us!" Catalina cried, tears brimming in her eyes.

"Yes, sweetie, I agree. But others may not. Time will tell soon enough. Don't worry about it. Okay?"

"Okay, Mother. But I can't stop thinking about it." Catalina continued as she wiped her tears.

Gateskin walked into the kitchen as his children were looking quite upset. "What's the matter? You should be jumping for joy with the latest news."

"We are happy, Father. But at the same time, we are worried about losing the dragon babies to Dragonaria," Catalina stated with a sniffle.

"I see. I will handle that, sweetheart. You do not need to concern yourself with this matter."

"But what if the dragon ladies of Dragonaria come here and try to take them away?" Serena persisted.

The dragon ladies had visited a few times in the past and were the ones to bring Madrigal and Izara to Sovorotskina from their island of Dragonaria.

"I won't let that happen. Now think about what names the dragons will have. Maybe Madrigal and Izara will need help picking names. You can offer to help them."

"We can, Father? Will they let us choose names?" Catalina began to jump around in joy.

"Well, I can't say for sure. You will have to ask them when the time comes."

"Okay. I can pick some really good names, Father," Catalina exclaimed.

Simon added, "Can I help pick names too, Father?"

"Of course, if the dragon parents need help. But it is up to them, not us which ones they choose. You can offer suggestions."

"Okay, we need to put our heads together, Serena and Catalina," Simon stressed.

Simon and Catalina raced off to their rooms to begin to converse about making lists of names right away.

Serena exchanged winks with her parents then joined her siblings shortly thereafter.

"Do you think that was a good idea, dear?" Solinara questioned.

"Well, it did perk them up a bit. Now they are not worrying about losing the dragons to Dragonaria."

"I guess that is one way to look at it, Gateskin. But I don't know if it was a good thing. The dragons may not like us interfering with name choices," Solinara sighed.

Unfortunately, there was someone creeping around the King's house when he heard this interesting news that intrigued him. He couldn't wait to spread the word.

# CHAPTER FOUR

The villagers of Sovorotskina gathered in the large square of the village and whispered back and forth. They couldn't believe what they had heard. They felt compelled to contact King Gateskin to confirm this rumor right away.

One of the elder villagers named Silas stepped forward and stated, "I will contact King Gateskin right away. I plan to visit him in person instead of trying to send a message his way. I know how busy a king he is, but this is a serious rumor that must be confirmed or denied as soon as possible. I know how you all feel about this. Your lives are in jeopardy if this is true."

The crowd agreed as they nodded their heads and yelled out their assents.

"I will be back as soon as I can and let you know what the King says. In the meantime, stay in your homes and watch over your children and livestock," Silas stated in a serious tone.

Silas wrapped his cloak around him and went back to his home to inform his wife that he would be back as soon as possible. He did not want her to worry about him. He instructed his eldest son to watch over his mother and his younger siblings and stay with them inside until his return.

***

Back at the home of Gateskin and Solinara, she peeked in at her children to see if they were still working on the names for the dragons. What she saw was comical to say the least. The three children were writing their own lists which were all a few pages long. She chuckled and moved away from their rooms to report to Gateskin.

Her husband was busy in the yard with the wolves making sure that they were in good health as he watched them race after Rabbinels. Solinara walked over to him and told him what she had seen.

"Well, I guess they will be kept busy and out of trouble for a while, dear."

"I guess so but what names could they possibly have come up with and so many? I don't see how the dragons are going to like this at all, especially Izara," Solinara chuckled.

Before Gateskin could respond, a villager came into view heading their way.

"Who is that, Gateskin?"

"It looks like Silas. He doesn't look happy though. I wonder what has happened in the village. I may have to visit there because he is looking at me."

"I pray no one is injured or sick," Solinara exclaimed.

"We will find out soon enough, Solinara. Why don't you go prepare some refreshments for him. He looks tired and thirsty."

"Of course, dear. I was thinking the same thing. Bring him inside with you. I am intrigued about what this is all about too."

"Don't worry. You will be informed fully, my dear," Gateskin winked at her and went to meet his visitor.

"Silas, it is good to see you, my friend. How are you and your family?"

Silas bowed and responded, "We are well, King Gateskin. But that is not what I came to see you about."

"I hope it is nothing too serious, Silas. You do look quite upset."

"I am."

"Well, let's go inside and sit down and discuss whatever is bothering you. Solinara is preparing some refreshments for you. You look like you need some."

"I could use a cup of the Queen's elderberry tea and a scone or two."

"Haha, of course, Silas. I know how you love her tea, cakes and scones."

Silas stepped inside and sat down at the table and sighed. After a few sips of tea and a bite of raspberry scone, he felt better and began to speak of what he had heard, "I was out in my garden pulling up some of the rooted vegetables before it got too cold when one of my neighbors came over to see me in a hurry. His face was flushed and he was sweating at the same time as if he had run a mile."

Gateskin nodded for him to continue.

"He said that he had heard word about something quite strange from some of the other villagers. They said that Botular, a former spy of King Kaposkaran of Parotovina, had told them this rumor. I didn't want to believe it. Well, you know Botular. He is trouble with a capital T."

"Yes, I agree, Silas. Now what did Botular tell them?"

"He said that there were going to be two more dragons being born in the village. Is this true, King?" Silas looked at Gateskin with a wide-eyed stare.

"Hmm, I see. This was told to everyone in the village by Botular?"

"Yes, that is what my neighbor said. Everyone knows about it. We all met in the square and shared our thoughts. That is why I am here to confirm or deny this rumor."

"Do you feel threatened by this, Silas? Do others feel that way too?"

"Well, yes, we all do. You already have two dragons and the idea of having two more is frightening. I know you have trained the two dragons but the new ones are not trained when they are born. How will you keep them away from all of us, especially our children and livestock?"

"I planned on discussing this with everyone soon, Silas. I didn't realize you would hear about it like this. I will have to see Botular about starting the rumor."

"But is it true, King Gateskin?"

"Yes, it is true, Silas. But there is no need for anyone to be concerned or frightened. I will have the dragonets under my control right away. Also, their parents will be training them to behave. I promise you."

"Oh my, I can't believe this! How did this happen?"

"Well, we all know how it happened, Silas," the King chuckled.

"Yes, yes, of course. I don't mean that. But I can't believe that it happened now. Did you realize that they could have offspring?"

"I didn't even think about something like this. I hadn't imagined it would ever happen. But we have something to be happy about, Silas. We will have four protectors against all the evil that Parotovina tries to spread here in Sovorotskina."

"I see. I guess you are correct, King Gateskin. I just need to get used to the fact and so will everyone else. What am I to say to the villagers when I return? Will we get to meet all four dragons?"

"You will not be responsible for saying anything to them. I will return with you and take care of everything. I don't want anyone to worry unnecessarily. As for meeting the dragons, I plan on introducing all the dragons to the village in time. Now enjoy your tea, cakes and scones. I will be right back."

Gateskin leaned over to whisper in his wife's ear, "Keep him here and I will return shortly after I have a visit with Botular."

Solinara nodded, smiled and sat down next to Silas with a plate of fresh cakes and scones and another pot of tea which brought a wide smile to the old man's face.

# CHAPTER FIVE

Botular was back in his cottage, sitting at the table enjoying his tea and cupcakes that the Queen had left for him the previous day. He had saved a couple of cupcakes to enjoy today. He smiled to himself that he had delivered the message to all the villagers. They were quite upset which gave him some pleasure.

He finished one cupcake and started on the other when he heard a knock at his door.

"Who is it?" he asked as the door opened and he saw the angry face of King Gateskin. This made him step away from the door and hang his head. He knew why the King was there. He had figured this would happen but didn't expect the rumor to reach the King so quickly.

"Botular, may I come in?" the King asked in a stern voice.

"Yes, of course, King. Please come in. Would you like some tea? I would offer you a cupcake but I finished one and started on the other one already."

"No thank you. I do not need any refreshments. This is not a social call, Botular."

He could feel the King's eyes boring into him as they took a seat at the table.

"I…I… think I know why you are here, King Gateskin."

"Do you, Botular?"

"Yes, I…I…am sorry for spreading the rumor about the dragons. I overheard you talking as I passed by. I didn't mean to cause any trouble."

"You didn't? You mean to say that you didn't realize what a stir this news would make to the villagers who are already afraid of the dragons?"

"Well, I thought that they would be happy to hear this news. They are anxious to meet the dragons and now there will be four of them."

"I think it is time for you to stay away from the villagers and mind your own business. Do you understand what I am saying, Botular?"

"Yes…yes, I do, King Gateskin. I apologize if I caused any problems by sharing this news. Does this mean that I am not allowed to leave my home?"

"Well, what do you think, Botular? Is there another way to stop you from causing any more trouble?"

"I…I…don't know. But I could promise not to do anything like this again, King," Botular begged.

"I could send you back to Parotovina. Would that be better?"

Botular came to Sovorotskina to spy on King Gateskin from King Kaposkaran from Parotovina where he was under the rule of this king as a guard and his eyes and ears. Botular was allowed to stay in Sovorotskina if he wanted to become a citizen and escape the tyranny of his former home. But he had to promise not to cause any trouble again or he would be banished back to Parotovina where he would be punished or even killed by King Kaposkaran for not fulfilling his duty as a spy.

"Oh no, no…please don't do that. I will stay at home until you say I can venture out again, King."

"All right. That is what you will do. Otherwise, if this happens again, I will be forced to send you back."

"I understand, King Gateskin. I truly understand. I am sorry if I caused anyone any harm. I won't do anything like this ever again!" Botular hung his head, not able to meet the King's eyes for fear of being zapped to dust or sent back to Parotovina.

"That is good to hear. I will be checking in with you from time to time. Make sure you keep your word, Botular. You know ***I*** always do!"

King Gateskin opened the door before Botular could say anything more and left, not looking back at the pale-faced man.

When Gateskin returned to his home, Solinara and Silas, the elder villager, were in deep discussion about all kinds of things but looked up when Gateskin entered.

He nodded at his wife and turned to Silas, "Are you ready to return home?"

"Yes, of course, King. I am fully refreshed and had a wonderful conversation with the beautiful Queen Solinara."

"I'm pleased to hear that. Well, let's go. I will carry you along for a quicker flight home. No need for you to walk all that way again."

"You will fly me home, King?"

"Yes, does that suit you?"

"Oh, yes, King. I am very happy to fly with you. I have never flown before. Will it be scary?"

The King did not answer but instead he picked up Silas and tucked him under his arm, lifted off and flew like the wind in the direction of the village square.

Silas gasped and held his breath and only breathed again once he was on land. He sighed heavily, breathed deeply, and smiled at the King in thanks. "That was quite a trip! I loved every minute of it! Thank you so much, King Gateskin."

"It was my pleasure, Silas. You will have something to share with your family, I'm sure."

"Oh yes. They won't believe it!" Silas went directly home to relate his adventure.

King Gateskin called out to the villagers. His voice carried magically over the wind and was heard at each house. Soon the villagers gathered in the square and waited to hear what their king had to say.

"My friends, I am here to explain about the rumor that was going around as related to me by Silas. I did not plan to tell you this soon but now that you have heard the news, I will share this with you."

"Do you mean, King, that the rumor is true?" one villager asked in alarm.

"Yes, it is true. Our dragons will soon be parents to two dragon babies or dragonets."

"Oh my! What are we going to do?" another asked.

"You need not do anything. I was planning on introducing you all to the four dragons eventually after I have had time to train them. You are not in any danger. I repeat. You are not in any danger. I will be training the new dragons as soon as possible along with their parents. They will be kept in their lair and watched over closely at all times. You need to stay in the village and away from the lair. I will announce when I plan to bring them to the village square for the introductions."

"Wow! We are going to finally meet the dragons? The little ones too?" a woman asked, surprised.

"Yes, you will meet all four dragons. I'm sure some of you have already seen me riding the dragons over the UT."

"Yes, King. I did see you fly over as well as some of my neighbors. We can't wait to see them up closer though as long as we are safe from harm," another man stated with a concerned expression.

"You are always safe as long as I am King here. I plan to always protect you with my own life."

"Thank you, King Gateskin. We can't tell you how important it is that we feel safe at all times," one woman expressed, anxiously.

"You have my word as always, Marion. Do you trust me?"

"Oh, of course, we trust you, King Gateskin. We would never doubt your word. We are thankful that you are our king. We wouldn't want anyone else to lead us."

"Good, then that is settled. You will wait to hear from me when the dragons are born. I will send word about their birth to all of you. It will be a time for celebration and thanksgiving because we will have more than enough protection from those who want to harm us. You all know who I speak of, don't you?"

"Most definitely we do, King," all answered in tandem.

"I will leave you now to think about all this. Share the news with others who are not here to hear my words. Just remember to stay away from the lair until I send word that I plan to bring them all to meet you here."

Cheers could be heard as the villagers dispersed and returned to their homes to share the exciting news of the upcoming births of the dragons with the rest of their families.

Gateskin flew back to his home where his wife was waiting to hear what transpired.

# CHAPTER SIX

Gateskin shared how the villagers responded to his announcement about the dragonets. She only had one question, which was surprising.

"Did they appear to be concerned about more dragons inhabiting our village?"

"Not really. But I'm sure they will have more concerns after they meet them."

"I see."

"Do you plan on visiting regularly with the dragons, dear?" Gateskin asked his wife.

"Well, I feel that I should check in from time to time with Izara to see how she is feeling and give her some of the new food that I have added the necessary nourishment she will need to support her two eggs."

"I will accompany you. I want to see how she is doing too, and how long it will be before she delivers her dragonets."

"Dragonets?"

"Yes, I guess you could call them that since the word means small dragons."

The King and Queen flew over to the lair to check on Izara. The dragon was lying down and fast asleep when they went inside after announcing to Madrigal that they were there to check on her. That was something they had to always remember to do – announce their presence. Dragons were very protective of their lair and could attack them. Though Gateskin did not feel threatened in any way.

Madrigal looked up at the King and Queen from where he was dutifully lying next to Izara to keep her warm.

"How is she doing today, Madrigal?" Queen Solinara inquired.

"She is tired all the time, Queen. I can't get her to move from here. She eats her food, drinks plenty of water and goes back to sleep. I wake her after a few hours and get her to relieve herself. I don't want her to mess up our sleeping area."

"Good thinking, Madrigal," King Gateskin replied with a soft chuckle for fear of waking her up.

"Don't worry about waking her. She sleeps like the dead. She hasn't had a problem sleeping before but has never slept this soundly," Madrigal announced.

Queen Solinara rested her hands on Izara's head and stomach area. She felt around for the tips of the eggs and then nodded. "She is doing well. They are growing fast and will be here before we know it. They appear to be quite large eggs. I hope she will not have a problem birthing them."

"What will happen if she does have an issue?" Madrigal asked with a frown of concern.

"I will be here to assist her. If you see that she is straining to push, call me right away. I have some herbs and potions to aid her in the delivery," she answered.

"Oh, thank you, kind queen. I don't know what we would have done without you if this happened on Dragonaria," Madrigal added.

"I'm sure she would have been fine if she had to deliver there," the Queen stated.

"Oh, maybe not! Especially if she was having a difficult time delivering. Other dragons would have attacked her and killed her and eaten the eggs if they saw that she was in trouble."

“Is that so?” Gateskin asked in surprise. He exchanged concerned looks with his wife.

“Yes, it is dragon eat dragon to survive there. Only the strongest and healthiest survive,” Madrigal announced sadly.

“It is safe for you here. Besides, I am always here for you, Madrigal. No need to worry. I guess becoming a father is a new thing for you. I understand. I think King Gateskin understands how you feel too, right Gateskin?” Solinara stated as she looked at her husband with a grin.

“Oh, I do know how you feel, Madrigal. I felt that way with all three of my offspring,” Gateskin guffawed.

“We will leave you now, Madrigal. I will return later with her new food and of course yours too,” Solinara responded with a smile.

Madrigal nodded and laid down once again protectively next to his mate.

The King and Queen quietly left the lair and flew back to their home musing over what

Madrigal had shared with them about his former home on Dragonaria.

"Do you think that is what would have happened to them if Izara had an issue delivering?" Solinara asked.

"It must be so or Madrigal wouldn't have mentioned it."

"Yes, I suppose. That is quite frightening to think about though," Solinara said with a shiver.

"I know, dear. Don't even think about it. They are here with us now and we will keep them safe," Gateskin responded with a smile to calm his wife down.

"Yes, I have to keep thinking that way. They are safe with us as well as we are safe with them."

Gateskin nodded but wore a solemn expression for he was concerned about what he had just heard too.

# CHAPTER SEVEN

On Dragonaria the dragon ladies, Aharona and Navaeha, were flying around with their dragons, Callum and Evander, respectively. They were looking for any sign of their elder sister, Elowen. They knew she must be up to something sinister as usual with her Dark Magic and potions that continue to threaten their island home. She had done things in the past to try to harm their parents by locking them up in the basement and another time nearly killing their father with a strong potion.

The dragon ladies were getting restless and were looking forward to visiting their friend, King Gateskin, on Sovorotskina again. They were trying to be as careful as possible around their parents who did not want them to return to Sovorotskina.

"Do you think that Father and Mother will be more attuned to us leaving here to visit King Gateskin again soon, Aharona?" Navaeha asked her older sister.

"I don't think they are as yet. But if we keep doing their bidding and don't cause any problems, I'm sure they will agree to letting us go."

“I certainly hope so, Aharona. I am getting bored flying around here. There is nothing to do. Our dragons are bored too. They miss seeing their friends, Madrigal and Izara.”

“Yes, I agree. I miss seeing them too. Let’s give it some more time and then we can ask our parents. In the meantime, do your jobs and keep an eye out for Elowen. We need to make sure she is behaving herself.”

“Okay, Aharona. But I haven’t seen or heard from her since her last escapades when King Gateskin was here to help us get Father back to good health. That potion Elowen gave him nearly killed him.”

“I think that is what she wanted to do so she could control Dragonaria.”

“Do you think she will try to kill us too? We are next in line for the throne,” Navaeha said with a quiver in her voice.

“No, I don’t think she would go so far as to kill us too. That is why we need to keep our eyes and ears open to anything she may be planning.

We can't go anywhere just yet. If we leave Father and Mother alone, Elowen might try something else. Each time we left to visit Sovorotskina, she did something."

"Oh, I didn't think of that, Aharona. Sorry. I can wait a little longer before we leave."

Jelitza, their cousin, flew up next to them on Verite, a smaller female dragon.

"What are you doing flying around in circles, cousins?"

"Hi Jelitza. We are on the lookout for any sign of Elowen. Have you seen her?" Aharona asked.

"No. She appears to be hiding out in her home. I saw Mianna in the woods nearby. She said she hasn't seen Elowen for a long time either."

"Well, this could mean that she is working on some new potions for her Dark Magic. That is not a good sign," Aharona stressed with concern.

"Maybe she is sick or something," Jelitza stated.

"I don't think she ever gets sick, cousin. She treats herself with some health potion to keep herself well," Navaeha said.

"How do you know that, Navaeha?" Aharona asked, puzzled.

"I saw her taking something more than once when she was on her tirades. It appeared to calm her down."

"Hmm, interesting," Aharona replied.

"Let's go visit the other dragons to see if there are any new ones born," Navaeha said with enthusiasm.

"Okay. I guess we could veer that way. We haven't seen them in a few weeks or so. Maybe we have some newly born. This is the time of year when they lay their eggs," Aharona stated with a smile.

"I love seeing the new dragonets. They are so cute and clumsy. They are just learning how to fly."

"Yes, they are adorable but can be dangerous. We need to keep a safe distance," Navaeha stressed.

"Don't worry, sister, our dragons will protect us."

"I hope so, Aharona. I certainly hope so." Navaeha looked around her anxiously when they arrived at the dragons' lairs and hid behind the brush, trees and rocks nearby.

***

Back in Sovorotskina things were moving along for the dragons. Izara had laid her eggs and was caring for them with tenderness and care. She kept turning them over and over to warm all sides as she snuggled next to them.

Madrigal stayed close by to keep watch and protect them if need be. He beamed the whole time as he oohed and aahed about his mate as she turned the eggs once again.

Queen Solinara had visited every day to see how the eggs were doing. King Gateskin peeked in from time to time also like an expectant father. This made Solinara giggle each time she saw him looking around the corner of the door of the lair.

Madrigal looked up with a silly grin on his face when he spotted the King. He waved his wing at him and settled back down next to his mate and the eggs. He never took his eyes off of them for long. He hadn't been eating as much as usual and he had rushed back and forth out of the lair to relieve himself afraid of missing the moment that his precious dragonets came into the world.

"How are you feeling Izara?" the Queen asked.

"I am tired, Queen Solinara. I am not sleeping very much. I take little naps but I don't want to miss when my darlings hatch."

"I can understand that, Izara. You and Madrigal should take turns sleeping. That way one of you would always be awake to alert the other when the big day comes."

"Yes, we have done that too. But we are both so tired of watching them that we have at times both fallen asleep at the same moment."

"Well, I can come and stay here for a little while so you can both get some sleep," Queen Solinara stated.

"Oh no, we couldn't ask you to do that, Queen. You have been so kind to us. I am ashamed at how I acted when we first arrived here. I am sorry for my rudeness."

"You don't have to apologize, Izara. I can understand how you felt back then. It was a strange new place with new masters. It is understandable."

"Thank you for understanding, Queen. I am grateful. Now you must return home to take care of your own family. I will have Madrigal alert you when the moment happens with either or both of my eggs."

"As long as you are sure, Izara. I will be waiting to hear the good news. We are all excited about this extraordinary news. Even the villagers are waiting to hear when the big day arrives."

"Oh my! Are they okay with having four dragons in their village?"

"Well, they were nervous at first. But now they are getting used to the idea and are waiting on pins and needles like the rest of us to meet you all."

"I look forward to meeting them and showing off our progeny."

Madrigal nodded eagerly at his mate's words. He was turning the eggs for Izara while she spoke with the Queen. He did it as tenderly as a large dragon could.

Queen Solinara smiled and nodded to the dragons as she turned and flew back to her home. She knew the children were waiting to hear if the dragonets had arrived.

Serena and her siblings were waiting at the door as their mother came in. She smiled and shook her head at them.

"Really? Not yet?" Catalina sighed.

"They will be here soon. Don't worry. Madrigal will tell us when they hatch."

"Okay, I guess. I just can't wait to see them. They are going to be so cute," Catalina gushed.

"Just remember, you cannot visit them unless you are with your father or me. They are wild creatures and will attack you. They don't know any better."

"Okay, Mother. We promise not to visit them on our own. Right?" Catalina responded as she looked at her brother and sister.

"I will make sure no one goes near them, Mother. I will keep them away until you say we can go here," Serena said in a strong voice as the eldest sibling.

"Thank you, Serena. Now go finish your chores. The animals need food in the barn and the wolves are looking a little restless. Bring over some Rabbinels in the cages and let them go for the wolves. I think they need exercise."

"Yes, Mother. Let's go, Simon and Catalina," Serena nodded to her siblings who sighed and followed.

# CHAPTER EIGHT

King Gateskin was surveying the village with Spindle as they flew side by side through the area bordering the UT. They also flew over Botular's house to make sure that he was not trying to escape again.

"Do you want me to check on him, King?" Spindle asked.

"No, I don't think we need to do that just yet. But keep an eye out on his house every so often. I want to fly over the UT and check to see if there are any more problems with the Catlings. I am sure that your fellow Sprites would have alerted me if there were any more sick ones running loose."

"Yes, King. I have kept in touch with them. They assured me that all is quiet there. In fact, the Catlings are hiding out. They must be frightened over what transpired with the Parotovinan guards and that potion. That was certainly a strange thing."

"I agree, Spindle. It was. I think Queen Beregina and King Kaposkaran will be cooking something up again soon, but for now, we are safe from their interference."

"How are the dragons doing?"

"Ahh, they are doing well keeping close watch over their eggs. It shouldn't be too long before they become parents for the first time."

"Madrigal must be so excited," Spindle surmised.

"Yes, they both are as well as the rest of us. I feel as if I am expecting another child or two."

"Haha, you are funny, King. But you will be their master after all and be responsible along with their parents to train them."

"Yes, that I will do. I may need your assistance after the eggs hatch, Spindle."

"Of course, King. Whatever you need me to do, I am here."

"I want to assure that no one comes near the lair. You will be responsible along with Mitteran and the rest of the guards to patrol the area in the village. Watch for anyone who is wandering around too close to the lair. I know they are all curious about hatching. But I will need time to train the dragonets in safety. I don't want any accidents or deaths."

"I will keep watch, I promise, King, as well as the rest of the men and my fellow Sprites."

"Good. I know I can entrust you to do all you can to make this a smooth transition. We don't know how these dragonets are going to react to people. They will be hungry and want to eat whatever they can put into their mouths."

"I agree. I was nervous about the dragons when they first arrived for that reason. I thought they were going to eat me."

"Haha, lucky for you, Spindle, they don't like to eat wood."

"Yep, I found that out. Madrigal told me and so did the dragon ladies' dragons. I think they all like me now," Spindle stated with a broad grin.

"Of course they like you, Spindle. They have seen you in action as a brave and courageous Head Guard."

"Well, I…." Spindle was speechless and turned a shade of green in embarrassment.

Before either could say another word, there was a cry in the distance.

"What was that?" Spindle asked, regaining his brown shade of color in his face.

"I don't know. Maybe it's the dragons. Let's go see."

The two flew over to the lair and looked inside after announcing they were there.

Madrigal was laying beside Izara and looking closely at the eggs.

"Is everything okay?" King Gateskin inquired.

"Oh, yes. Nothing happening yet," Izara answered.

"We heard a cry in the distance and thought it was time for the hatching."

Madrigal answered, "No, King. We didn't cry out. I thought I heard something too. But we have been so busy turning the eggs and gazing at our dragonets that we didn't pay too much attention to the noise."

Suddenly there was another cry. King Gateskin flew out of the lair and looked around along with Spindle.

"Where did that come from, Spindle?"

"I will fly over to the UT and ask the Sprites. They might have heard something and know in what direction it came from."

King Gateskin flew over to Botular's house to check on him. All was quiet there though. He peered in the windows and saw Botular sleeping.

He checked the house of the Quintaroons, men who were changed into creatures with a potion by Queen Beregina of Parotovina, but found them sleeping also.

These Quintaroons were now men after Gateskin changed them back with a spell of his own. He had to keep careful watch over these men to ensure that they did not endanger his village if they changed back into their creature forms. Spindle and Mitteran were in charge of keeping tabs on these men at all times because in the past they had tried to escape from their home.

The Quintaroons had come to Sovorotskina on a mission to wreak havoc at the request of King Kaposkaran. Gateskin stopped them from doing that and offered them asylum in his village if they vowed to behave. He still didn't trust them entirely but they had proven to be helpful when he needed their skills in a tight situation.

Next, he flew over to Jennara's and Henno's home, powerful people who had immigrated from Parotovina. They were working in their garden and looked up when the King flew down to them.

"What a pleasure to see you, King," Henno announced as he came forward to shake the King's hand.

"It's nice to see you both too. Unfortunately, this is not a social call. I came over to find out if you had heard a cry."

"A cry? No, sorry we didn't hear anything, King Gateskin. We were so busy in the garden and talking to each other," Henno replied, and Jennara nodded in agreement.

"Do you need our assistance, King?" Jennara asked.

"No, but please keep an ear out in case you hear anything. Just let me know."

"We will, King. Sorry we couldn't be a help to you."

The King nodded and flew to see his Wizards in their house nearby.

He knocked on the door and waited. He could hear some shuffling and noise coming from inside. He called out to them through their minds to get their attention.

The door opened quickly after that and the four Wizards stood there looking disheveled and exhausted.

"What's going on here?" the King asked. "Did you cry out?"

"Oh, King. Yes, sorry. We have been having a difficult time keeping the chest inside the vault we created to contain the beams. They keep trying to escape," Marno, Head Wizard, announced in agitation.

The chest was discovered in Mt. Ailylene after being buried there over 100 years ago by a wizard who wanted to keep the powers of the chest and what it held from an evil wizard. It purported to contain a powerful medallion that would bestow powers onto another if it was discovered by a wizard.

Gateskin stood outside the vault and looked deep inside to where the chest was sitting but not quietly. It was bouncing around up and down and side to side.

He laid his hands on it and it immediately quieted. He pulled the chest out of the vault and put it on the table as the four Wizards gathered close by.

"What are we to do with it, King?" Marno asked.

"Well, it appears to be trying to tell us something. Maybe if we ask it a few questions it will answer somehow," Gateskin replied.

"What should we ask for, King?" Fortag, second Wizard quizzed. Wizards three and four, Wassor and Tornak nodded and waited for the King to respond.

"We need to know what it wants, first of all. Let's see what it will do," Gateskin replied.

The King held the chest in his hands and spoke to it. "What do you want?"

He waited for several seconds with no reply or movement.

Gateskin tried again, "What is it that you want to tell us?"

The chest began to vibrate in the King's hands. He placed it down on the table and waited.

The beams of light shone brightly through the chest walls and lit the room in a golden glow. It stayed this way for a few minutes and then the beams went out taking the golden light in the room with them.

"What is it you want?" King Gateskin asked once again.

The beams shone brightly throughout the room sending a tapping sound on the table like a code.

The Wizards came closer and began to record the taps that came repeatedly, some close others farther apart.

"What is it trying to tell us?" Wassor asked.

"Wait a minute," Marno expressed in impatience. "I'm trying to record this."

"I think it is trying to give us a warning," Tornak responded in alarm.

"Yes, I think so too," Fortag said as his face blanched.

"It is a warning. It said that its master is coming back to claim the beams," Marno explained.

"When is this going to happen?" King Gateskin asked the chest.

The chest tapped out its code and became silent.

"The wizard who is to claim the chest is already here!" Marno exclaimed in shock.

# CHAPTER NINE

Gateskin looked at the chest in alarm as his Wizards stared at him with wide-eyes full of fear, something he never had seen on them before.

"We will not concern ourselves with this until we need to, Wizards," the King announced in a strong voice meant to allay the Wizards' fears.

"But…what are we to do to protect ourselves and the village?" Marno asked, his voice shaky for the first time.

"If this wizard is here, he or she will announce their presence to us soon enough. We must open this chest even if we release the beams. First, we will put it back into the vault and put a cover around it that will contain the beams and keep them from escaping as they did previously," the King explained.

"Okay, let's get to work, Wizards," Marno commanded, sounding more assured.

The four Wizards bent over the chest and began to chant to prepare a cover over the chest to contain the beams as they worked to open the chest and remove whatever was in there, hopefully the Medallion.

Gateskin left them to complete their tasks. He was going to survey his land and find Spindle and Mitteran to assist him. He would make sure that no one or wizard would harm his people.

Spindle came as soon as he heard the King's summons along with Mitteran close behind.

"What is wrong, King?" Spindle asked, his brow wrinkled in concern.

"We came as soon as we heard your summons, King," Mitteran added.

"Thank you both. You are good men." Gateskin explained what had just transpired with the chest.

"Do you think that there is a wizard hiding out here in the village?" Spindle questioned.

"I don't know yet. I have feelers out and I am looking throughout the UT but cannot see anything," King responded, continuing to survey the land.

As they all flew over the village and the UT, they whispered back and forth that all was clear.

A voice was heard calling the King's name. Gateskin looked down and saw a lone figure.

He flew down to greet the individual who had called out to him.

"What are you doing roaming around, Arubane?"

Arubane is the adopted son of Hotenfaran and Procelina, brother and sister-in-law to the Queen.

Wearing a frown, Arubane asked, "I heard someone calling out to me. Was that you, King Gateskin?"

"No, Arubane. I did not call you. Where are your parents?"

"They are at home at the moment. We just came back from our travels around Noella Province. They were selling their wares and looking for some new products to purchase for our potions."

"Oh, I see. I'm sure they will be able to let me know that they are back."

"Yes, we planned to visit soon. They have much to share with you from our travels."

"Good to hear. I look forward to seeing them and you too. My children will be happy to hear that you are back. They have missed you and your parents."

"I've missed them too. I am excited to share some new incantations that I have developed." Arubane smiled and shook his head and then frowned.

"What's wrong, Arubane?" the King asked.

"I keep hearing someone summoning me to come. They are saying something about, 'It is time to claim it!'"

"What are you supposed to claim, Arubane?"

"I don't know. It is getting louder and making me walk this way."

"Keep moving. We will follow you," the King urged him forward.

"You can fly with us, Arubane. I know you can do that," Gateskin stated with a grin. "You can call me uncle, you know."

"Yes, I do know how to fly, King Gateskin. I don't feel right calling you uncle though."

King Gateskin nodded and welcomed Arubane to lead the way.

Spindle, Mitteran, and the King flew along with Arubane as he led the way to the house of the four Wizards.

# CHAPTER TEN

King Gateskin and his entourage exchanged confused expressions as they landed outside the Wizards' home.

"Is this where you feel the messages are coming from, Arubane?"

"Yes, King. I feel them very strongly now as I stand here. They are almost yelling at me now. What and who is this?"

"I don't know, Arubane, but we will find out soon. Let's go in."

King Gateskin knocked on the door and waited for the Wizards to come forward. He was sure they would have an explanation for these messages.

Marno opened the door and looked surprised to see the King, Head Guards, and Arubane standing on his doorstep. He waited for the King to explain his appearance so soon after leaving there.

"Marno, may we come in? We need to speak with you about an incident."

"Of course, King. Please come in," Marno responded as he bowed and stepped aside to allow all visitors entrance. His fellow Wizards looked confused also and waited to hear what this was all about.

King Gateskin began to explain, "This young man is Arubane. I think you already know who he is. He is quite a talented wizard in his own way. He just relayed something to me. I will let him explain." Turning to Arubane he pushed him forward to begin.

"I am honored to be in your home, Wizards. I have been receiving messages coming from this house since I returned home from my trip with my parents all over Noella Province. The messages are getting stronger and are now so loud that they are alarming and hurting my ears."

"What messages are you receiving, Arubane?" Marno asked.

"The first message was 'You must claim it. Come immediately and stake your claim."

"What are you supposed to claim?" Fortag, second Wizard quizzed.

"Well, that I don't know. It seems to think that I know what it is speaking of each time."

“That doesn’t make any sense if you don’t know what it means,” Wassor expressed.

King Gateskin moved over to the vault to look in at the chest. It was glowing and bouncing around.

The four Wizards hurried over to observe this strange occurrence.

“What is happening here, King?” Marno asked.

The three other Wizards looked over the shoulders of the King and Marno to see what was causing this disturbance in the vault.

Arubane’s face paled and he looked as if he was going to pass out. He struggled to stand in one place until Fortag noticed his discomfort and assisted him to a chair where he sighed heavily and then passed out.

King Gateskin rushed to Arubane’s side and waved a hand over his face to wake him. “What happened there, Arubane?”

“I don’t know. I felt the strength of something pulling me forward and I refused to move but it kept clawing at me inside and outside my body."

"Did you hear any messages before you passed out?" the King asked.

"No, just a pulling sensation that would not let me go."

"Okay, just sit still and I will stay with you until you feel strong enough to move," Gateskin stressed.

"I feel strong, King. I just don't know what it wants of me? I don't understand any of this."

"Don't worry, Arubane. We will figure it out," the King replied.

He turned toward his Wizards and spoke to them in their minds to come up with an explanation of what just happened. He suspected that the chest was trying to contact Arubane for some strange reason.

Marno responded silently through his mind, "I think that Arubane is somehow connected to the wizard who buried this chest. What else could it be?"

"I agree but don't see how that is possible," King Gateskin replied.

"Do we know all of his history, King?" Wassor asked.

"We do know that his parents were wizards in their own rights. They were powerful people who kept their powers undercover from King Parotovina."

"What do we know about his grandparents?" Fortag queried further.

"That I will have to find out," Gateskin answered. "I will have to ask his parents who adopted him. They may know something else."

"Is there anything else we can do to help you, King Gateskin?" Marno asked as he continued to study Arubane.

"No. I will get back to you as soon as I know more. Keep an eye on the chest and lock it inside the vault until I talk to you again. Let me know if it does anything else like it did now."

"Yes, of course, King. We will keep careful watch over it," Marno responded as his fellow Wizards nodded in agreement.

The King and his entourage left the Wizards' home keeping watch over Arubane as they flew the young man home to see his parents.

Hotenfaran and Procelina were outside their home when the King arrived with Arubane. Arubane's parents looked up as they saw Arubane flying overhead with the King and his guards.

Procelina took one look at her son and cried out, "What happened to him? Is he sick or something?"

"He does look very pale. Where have you been, Arubane?" Hotenfaran asked his son with deep concern, furrowing his heavy brows.

"I am all right now, Father and Mother. You need not worry," Arubane sighed as he sat down on the front steps of his home.

Hotenfaran looked at King Gateskin and waited for an explanation.

"We need to speak privately, Hotenfaran," King Gateskin began and continued to explain what had happened to Arubane.

"Are you telling me that he is somehow related to either the evil wizard who searched for it or the good wizard who buried the chest with the Medallion?"

"We don't have any other explanation for these messages coming to him."

# CHAPTER ELEVEN

Catalina whispered to her brother, Simon, "What if we go sneak a peek at the dragonet eggs? I can blend into my surroundings and bring you with me."

"Can you make sure that I am completely covered too?" Simon asked in a shaky voice.

"Sure. I have done this before. Don't you remember when we were in Crotesia Mountain hiding from the Parotovina guards, the time we were looking for Father?"

"Oh, right. I remember now, Catalina. But it wasn't safe then and it certainly isn't safe now."

"Maybe. But we won't stay long. I just want to take a look at the eggs. They could be hatching now as we speak."

"Well, I don't feel right about this. Are you going to tell Serena?"

"No on your life, Simon. She will snitch and tell Father and Mother and stop us."

"I guess so. But I don't know about this, Catalina. If Mother and Father find out about this, we will be punished."

"I am brave. Aren't you brave, Simon?"

"Of course I am brave. I will do it."

"Hurray! Let's go now before anyone sees us. You can fly us there, right?"

"Of course I will! I plan to do that!" Simon grumbled and frowned at his sister.

They snuck out of the house and flew into the air where Catalina put an invisibility cloak around them making them disappear in mid-air.

At the lair Madrigal was keeping close tabs on his mate and the eggs which were moving around more but not cracking open yet. It appeared that the dragonets were getting antsy and almost ready to escape their shells.

The dragons were unaware that there were two other bodies hovering over their heads as they entered the lair and looked down on the eggs.

Madrigal felt a breeze and looked around and up to see where it was coming from. "Hmm, did you feel that, Izara?"

"No, I didn't feel anything. What do you mean, Madrigal?"

"Well, I felt a breeze around us. I don't know where it was coming from though."

"Never mind that, Madrigal. Look!"

Izara held her breath as she cried out again, "Look what is happening!'

Madrigal looked closely at the eggs and sniffed them. "It looks like they are getting ready to hatch, my love."

"Yes, they are hatching!! I can't believe it! We are going to be parents, Madrigal, very soon!"

Simon and Catalina gazed down in wonder. They tried to keep their voices from crying out. "Look at what is happening, Simon! We arrived just in time!" Catalina exclaimed in bewilderment.

"I can see that, Catalina. I guess we did. We can't stay here too long though. We must get back home before they discover us. I don't think the dragons will be happy that we are here."

Catalina looked at the eggs as they hatched and soon a leg or claw could be seen coming out and pecking at the shell to open it further.

She gasped in surprise to see the bright yellow color of the dragon who was struggling to come into the world. It was so beautiful she almost yelled out loud.

"Ooh, look at it, Simon! It is so beautiful!"

"Yes, it is like looking at the sun. It is so bright! Wow!"

"It also has some turquoise like Izara on its head. Do you see that?"

"Yes, it looks like its mother!" Simon gushed.

"The other egg is hatching too, Simon! It has a red and purple head like its father."

"They are so beautiful! Cute, too!"

"Now we must get back before they discover we are here," Simon pressed on.

"I know, but let me watch them until they come out of their shells completely," Catalina insisted as she couldn't keep her eyes off of the dragonets.

The dragonets were almost completely out of their shells as they pecked at the last of the shell that stuck to their scales. Their parents helped them by cleaning them up and licking them all over.

The children began to move out of the lair but could feel the dragonets looking up at them. The dragonets couldn't fly yet but were trying to reach up toward them.

"What are they doing, Madrigal?" Izara observed their dragonets trying to fly up and reach something above them.

Madrigal looked upward and didn't see anything but kept watching the air move around them and again felt a breeze that grew in intensity as the children flew out of the lair and back home to safety.

The children giggled all the way home as they excitedly kept sharing the moments of the hatching.

"You do know that we cannot share this with anyone or we will have to pay for disobeying our parents."

"I know, Simon. I won't be the one to tell anyone," Catalina bragged as she wore a smile of satisfaction.

Simon responded, "Yeah, right!"

They became visible before they arrived home but landed away from their house so no one would see them sneaking back.

What they didn't notice was their elder sister, Serena, had spotted them landing as she was feeding the animals in the barn. She moved toward them and planned to find out what they were up to before their parents found out.

She came out of the barn and called out to them, "What are you two planning?"

Catalina and Simon jumped back in alarm. They looked at each other and wore expressions of distress.

"See, I told you we would be caught!" Simon said, with a heavy sigh.

They looked up at their sister with wide eyes full of anxiety as she headed their way.

***

While the children were watching the eggs hatch there were two Quintaroons who were sniffing the air at the windows of their house.

"Do you smell that, Quintal?" Taron asked.

"Hmm, yet, I do. It smells tasty, doesn't it?"

"I agree. Do you think it is the dragons? I heard the villagers talking as we took a walk with Spindle about the dragons having two eggs that were going to hatch."

"Yes, I heard that too, Taron. I am waiting for the King to come and visit us and keep us locked up again."

No sooner did they say this but the King was at their door.

"Ahh, King. So nice to see you. Are you going to share the news about the new dragonets coming?" Quintal dared to ask.

"Well, as a matter of fact, I am. I know that you were out recently with Spindle. He shared that you had heard the rumors about the dragons expecting."

"Yes, we have. Intriguing. We can't wait to see the little critters. Can we, Taron?"

Taron nodded but kept his eyes away from the King's fiery stare.

"It is time to keep you under lock and key again until it is safe for you to venture out."

"But we can take care of ourselves, King Gateskin, especially if we change into our other selves."

"Yes, Quintal. That I am aware of and that is the very reason you will stay inside until I say it is safe for you to leave your home. Spindle will come visit you often and bring your food."

"But when will we be able to leave and take our walks again?"

"There will be plenty of time for that. After I complete the training of the dragonets, you will be informed and given a time table for your strolls."

"I guess we have no other choice, do we?" Taron muttered in disappointment.

"That is correct. Now I must leave you. I have other places to go."

"Oh, King? When will the dragonets hatch?" Quintal asked.

"They will be here soon," the King replied with a wide grin.

# CHAPTER TWELVE

Madrigal quickly flew over to alert the King and Queen of the hatching of the eggs and delivery of his dragonets. He was so full of joy that he couldn't stop laughing out loud. He promised Izara to return as quickly as he could to help her keep the dragonets in line. They were hungry and needed some food as soon as possible or they would try to eat their parents.

Gateskin looked up from the wolves' den to see Madrigal heading his way with exaggerated sweeps of his enormous colorful wings sending waves of wind toward him and in every direction and rainbows as the light bounced off his scales.

The King flew to meet the excited dragon who was beaming from scale to scale.

"Well, this must mean that you have good news to share with me, Madrigal."

"Oh, yes, King. The time has arrived! We are officially parents of two dragonets!"

"Congratulations! I am so happy to hear this! I will get Solinara to bring some food for you and your family right away. I know they will be ravenous."

"Yes, they definitely are! I don't want to leave Izara too long or they may try to eat her!"

"Head back and we will follow right behind you."

Gateskin flew over to Solinara who was inside her workshop already preparing food for the new dragonets. She had picked up the words that Gateskin had sent to give her a heads-up. She grinned in delight to hear the news. She had anticipated the arrival and hoped that the dragonets were healthy. She shoved more food into large bags and lifted them up with a little magic and flew up to meet Gateskin who was waiting outside their home.

They swiftly flew over to the dragons' lair and landed outside announcing their arrival. They heard a lot of scuffling inside the lair. They peeked inside and saw the dragonets trying to fly around as their parents were pushing them back down. The dragonets' movements were erratic and clumsy. Their wings were not fully opened. Their parents did not want them to escape and get into all kinds of mischief.

Madrigal sighed in relief when he saw the King and Queen with bags full of food for them and their offspring.

The dragonets sniffed the air and the bags that were at their feet now. They tore at the bags eating all the food and the bags too in a few gulps. They looked up and burped, causing their parents and the King and Queen to laugh out loud.

Izara wiped their faces, licking away the leftover food. She nibbled at her own food as did Madrigal keeping eyes on their offspring at all times not only from love but also from fear that they would harm themselves or someone else.

The dragon parents had discussed what names they wanted for their offspring but once they saw how bright the female dragonet was, the name they had chosen didn't fit her. When Madrigal spotted the male dragonet, he knew right away what his name would be because he looked fierce.

Madrigal finished eating and introduced their dragonets to the King and Queen, "This is Sunniva which means sun gift. She will learn how to bow to you. I will teach her right away to do that." Madrigal bowed and prodded Sunniva to bow too. Sunniva looked confused but was forced to bow as her father kept his claws on her back.

Izara introduced the second dragonet, "This is Lorcan which means fierce. He will also learn to show reverence to you both. It will be the first lesson they will learn, King and Queen." Izara bowed to them and pushed Lorcan to do the same. Lorcan bopped up and down and turned upside down trying to show his strength.

"You will bow in reverence, Lorcan, and no funny business. Do you hear me?" Madrigal stressed as he growled at his son.

The King and Queen chuckled at Lorcan's antics and came forward to pet him on the head with Madrigal's claws holding the dragonet in place so he wouldn't harm them.

Sunniva came forward and put her head down so that Gateskin and Solinara could pet her too. She wore a smile as only a dragonet could smile showing her small teeth which surely would grow along with her.

Izara smiled too at seeing how well Sunniva responded to the King and Queen. Lorcan was another matter. He would be a challenge for sure. She surmised.

"We are so happy to meet you both, Lorcan and Sunniva. We will be spending a lot of time together soon. We will bring you more food when you let your parents know that you are hungry."

The two dragonets nodded, growled and burped again in anticipation of more food.

"I will return home to prepare more food for you, Lorcan and Sunniva. Sleep well now. You will both need plenty of that to grow strong," Queen Solinara stated.

Izara patted her dragonets' heads and pushed them to lay down to take a nap. It didn't take long for the dragonets to close their eyes and snore loudly.

Gateskin and Solinara flew home to share the good news with their children and soon after with the villagers who were anxious to hear.

Serena and her siblings were sitting in their play room waiting for their parents to arrive home. Catalina and Simon had confessed to Serena what they had done and were hanging their heads dreading the time they had to tell their parents the same thing.

Solinara called out to the children as she opened the door with Gateskin close behind. She was so excited to share this special moment with them. She moved from room to room and found them in the play room sitting around looking glum.

"What is the problem here? I have some good news that will turn their frowns upside down."

Serena stood up and went to hug her mother. "Please share the news with us, Mother." She eyed her siblings behind her mother's back and shook her head putting a finger to her lips to keep them quiet.

Catalina and Simon nodded and stood up to hug their mother too. "Please tell us the news, Mother."

"Well, the dragonets have arrived. We have a male named Lorcan with red and purple scales and a female named Sunniva with yellow and turquoise scales. They are just gorgeous and so sweet! We fed them and they actually bowed to us already with their parent's help," Solinara giggled.

"Wow! That is wonderful, Mother. We can't wait to meet them! They already have names? We thought we were going to share our names with the dragons," Catalina gushed, then grumbled in discontent.

"Well, evidently they already had some names in mind," Solinara stated.

"They are the parents, after all, children," Gateskin added with a grin. "Maybe if they have any more dragonets, you can make some suggestions."

"More? Will they have more dragonets, Father?" Simon asked, eagerly.

"Oh, Gateskin, really? I certainly hope they don't. Where are we going to keep more dragons?" Solinara sighed in exasperation.

Gateskin laughed out loud and shrugged his shoulders. "You never know."

The children laughed along with him and hugged him, dancing around in celebration.

"When can we go visit them, Father?" Serena asked, anxiously.

"We left them sleeping soundly after they filled their bellies. Maybe tomorrow you can all go with us when we deliver their food. We need to give them some space. They are youngsters and need plenty of sleep like you all did when you were young."

"I guess so, Father. But we are excited about meeting them," Catalina expressed with a wide smile and sparkling eyes.

"Yes, I know you are, sweetheart. Why don't you go help your mother get the food ready for all the animals. It is about time for their lunch. After that you can feed the wolves and other animals in the barn before we eat our own lunch."

"Yes, Father," Simon and Catalina sighed as they trudged along to their mother's workshop.

Serena patted them on their heads as they passed by her and said, "I will be along to help soon after I talk to Father."

"What?" Simon turned back and asked, wearily.

"Nothing important, Simon. I just need to find out more about the dragonets. I will share what I learn. Okay?"

Simon nodded and sighed as he left the house.

Catalina looked at her brother before they entered the workshop to help their mother. "Do you think she is going to tell them what we did?"

"No, I think she will keep our secret."

"I hope so. I know both our parents will be terribly upset with us and most likely forbid us from seeing the dragons at all," Catalina stated with tears in her eyes.

"Don't cry, Catalina. It will be okay. I trust Serena."

"If you say so, Simon," Catalina responded as she wiped away the tears before they could fall.

# CHAPTER THIRTEEN

Solinara was listening in on her children's conversation. She sighed and continued on with preparing the food as Catalina and Simon entered her workshop. She did not plan on telling them that she heard them speaking about something they had done. She would find out soon enough what this thing was. She knew that eventually they would not be able to keep it to themselves.

"Mother, we are here to help you. Father told us to feed the wolves and barn animals. Can we take a bag of this food?" Simon asked, as he entered the shop, not meeting his mother's stern eyes for she was looking at him in a strange way.

Catalina came along and lent a hand to her brother and picked up one of the filled bags for the wolves and another one for the other animals.

The two children left the workshop and proceeded to the wolves' huts.

Once outside, Simon looked at Catalina and whispered, "Did you see the way Mother looked at us?"

"What?" Catalina answered.

"I said, did you see the way Mother looked at us when we went into her workshop?"

"No, I really didn't notice. I was just watching her as she created the dragonets' food. She is amazing, don't you think?"

"Yeah, sure. But I can't believe you didn't notice her eyes. They looked so…so strange. I think she knows what we did."

"How could she? Serena didn't tell her and we certainly are not going to say a thing,"

"Don't you understand, Catalina? Mother is a powerful fairy and can surmise things without us saying a word. She is probably reading our minds now."

"What? I am not thinking about what we did. I promise I won't think about that," Catalina stressed, as she looked around her as if to see her mother standing there.

The two finished feeding the wolves and moved on to the barn to take care of the cow, pig, chickens and horse.

Serena had already milked the cow that morning so Milly was looking happy as she ate her food. Hank, the horse, had been walked around the area and was snoozing standing up as he chewed his food in his sleep.

The pigs were in their pen, and the chickens had their own enclosure away from the other animals.

Simon fed the pigs while Catalina took care of the chickens and swooped in to fetch the eggs while the hens were eating. They didn't always like someone touching their nests.

The two children were so busy that they didn't hear Serena enter the barn and enclosures.

"Are you two finished with your chores yet?" Serena asked.

"Oh, you startled me," Catalina said as she hurried to fetch a few more eggs. "I didn't hear you coming in here."

Simon turned and said, "Did you tell Father?"

"No, I told you both I made a promise to you to keep your secret even though you were both wrong and could have been in danger."

“Do you think so?” Simon asked, with some hesitation to say anything more.

“Yes, I do. Never do something like that again. Promise me!” Serena stressed, hands on hips and a fiery look in her eyes.

“Oh boy! You look like Mother when you do that, Serena!” Catalina giggled.

“I am serious! You must promise me. I will not cover for you next time,” Serena responded even more sternly.

“Okay, I’m sorry, Serena. We promise, right, Simon?” Catalina sighed.

Simon nodded and sighed in relief. “I knew you would support us. Thank you.”

“Time to eat lunch. Father sent me in to get you. Mother is still busy making the food so we have to make our own lunch. Let’s go.”

***

Back at the dragons' lair the dragonets were still sleeping with Izara by their side while Madrigal was flying around at the top of the lair thinking about the wind that was around them as the eggs hatch. He knew that someone had been there to observe the delivery, but who? It felt like it had been more than one person.

He knew that it wasn't the King or Queen but could it be one of the royal children? Could they blend into their surroundings? He knew that they were a powerful family.

He finally cleared his head and lay down next to his mate and dragonets to rest. Once they were up, he knew they would exhaust him with their energy. He must be getting old, he thought with a deep sigh. As he fell asleep the last thing on his mind was, could it have been Botular?

# CHAPTER FOURTEEN

Botular, now a citizen of Sovorotskina, was locked in his house but knew something was up. He could feel it in the air. If only he could figure out a way to escape and find out what was going on.

The King had not been back to see him for a day or two. Though there was food on the table for his breakfast, lunch and dinner at the right times, he couldn't remember seeing anyone come and go in his house. His food had somehow magically appeared.

He had enough left over from dinner the night before to finish for breakfast but now he was hungry for lunch. He looked out his windows and could see people moving around in the distance. They looked like they were celebrating something.

***

Gateskin had spent some time with the villagers to announce the birth of the dragonets. The villagers were now celebrating their birth by dancing and praying that the new dragonets would be healthy and not a danger to any of them.

Gateskin reiterated, "Listen, everyone. The dragons are taking care of their offspring and will keep them contained until they are safe to move around. They will never be alone to cause any of you to be concerned.

He then told them, "You will be happy to hear that the young dragons actually bowed to the Queen and I right after we met. How do you like that?"

The villagers shouted out their support and relief at this.

"I will always keep you safe. That is my promise, and you know I always keep my promises."

Silas stepped forward and said, "Yes, King Gateskin, we know what an honorable leader you are. We trust you to do what you say you will do, and that is to watch over us. Always."

Others nodded and cheered at Silas's words which brought the King to smile widely at this man, "Thank you, Silas. You are a good man yourself."

King Gateskin held up his hands and said, "Soon I will come back here with the dragons and their offspring to introduce you. But for now, I have much work to do to get them ready for a trip like that."

"We understand, King, don't we?" Silas asked his fellow villagers who nodded in reply.

"Well, I need to get back to check on them. I have much work to do to keep us all safe in our beautiful land. Please go back to your homes. I'm sure you have much to do too."

Silas directed the others to go home and back to work and wait until it was time for them to meet the dragons.

King Gateskin watched them walk away and flew back to his own home. He met his wife flying toward him with a tray of food.

"Do you need me to help you with that? Where are you going?"

"No, I am bringing lunch to Botular. Do you want to come with me to check on him? Maybe you want to be the one to announce the news."

"Hmm, good idea. He is probably wondering what all the noise and celebrating was about in the village. Their voices carried far and wide, I'm afraid. I just hope no one in the rest of the province heard them."

"I think it might be time to tell the other villages all about these creatures. They will find out soon enough," Solinara suggested.

"Yes, dear. I agree. Let's pay a visit with Botular first."

Botular was waiting at his door when he saw the King and Queen flying toward his house. He opened it before they could knock with the help of the King.

"Ahh, here you are. I was wondering when you would come with my lunch. I am starving!" Botular stated, looking disgruntled and neglected.

"We did not forget you, Botular," Queen Solinara said as she placed his warm plate in front of him on the table.

"Mm, it smells wonderful. I love your beef stew, Queen!" Botular said as he dug in without waiting another second.

The King and Queen exchanged looks but waited until Botular had finished his food.

"You don't have to stay here. I know you are busy with whatever is going on around here," Botular stated as he looked at them with a questioning stare.

"We were planning on coming here to not only bring your lunch but also to share the good news," King Gateskin began.

Botular waited expectantly for the King to continue.

"We now have two dragonets on our land. They hatched yesterday."

"I knew it! I knew there was something going on. I could hear some celebrating going on in the village. Their voices carried all the way to my house."

"I had a feeling that others may have heard this too," King responded.

"Do you fear that the wrong ones may now know this news, King?"

Gateskin met Botular's questioning eyes. "Yes, I think others may have heard the news already. But I do not fear that or anything else."

"Oh, sorry, King. I didn't mean to say that you were a fearful king. I didn't mean that at all. Please forgive me." Botular stressed this point, afraid that he would not be able to leave his house ever to meet the dragonets for that careless remark.

"I understand what you meant, Botular. No worries. You still have to prove that you can be trusted. I don't think you are ready to meet the dragonets, nor is anyone else. They need to be trained first."

"You read my mind, King. I have to be careful what I think."

"Yes, I did. I can do that with everyone, not just you. I will come back when it is time to introduce you. For now, you can go out and take your walks but stay away from the lair. Do you understand? Spindle will go with you."

"Oh, yes, King. I understand perfectly. Can I go into the village?"

"Only if you can behave yourself and not spread any other rumors."

"Oh, I learned my lesson, King. I will never do that again. I have missed moving around outside and visiting people and getting some fresh air."

"That is all you will do, Botular, get some fresh air and visit some friends in the village."

"Yes, King Gateskin. Thank you." Botular bowed to the King and Queen as he watched them leave his home.

He looked around and noticed that his plate was gone. Luckily, he had finished his food before it had vanished. He sighed happily.

# CHAPTER FIFTEEN

"Do you trust Botular to behave himself, Gateskin?" Solinara asked.

"I will keep him in my sights, no worries, dear. I will never completely trust Botular. Once a spy, always a spy."

"I agree, Gateskin," Solinara chuckled. "Do you think that King Kaposkaran still has some control over him?

"No, I don't think Kaposkaran even gives him a thought nowadays. But I will be keeping an eye out on Botular and so will Spindle and Mitteran for any trouble." Gateskin sent a message as such to Spindle and Mitteran who responded in kind to keep Botular under tabs.

Back at their home, Gateskin went directly to his Conference Room to contact his good friend, King Cavelan of Votovia, which bordered Sovorotskina to the west. He and Cavelan were close friends and shared all their problems and solutions to these problems.

Gateskin waited for the window to open and smiled when he saw his friend's face smiling back at him.

"My friend, how are you? I have been wondering when I would hear from you. I know how much is going on over there and didn't want to disturb you," Cavelan announced.

"Feel free to contact me anytime. I always welcome hearing from you, Cavelan. I wanted to share my good news with you first before I told the other rulers."

"Oh, I think I know what that is!" Cavelan answered in excitement.

"You do?" Gateskin asked in surprise.

"Yes. You opened the chest and have the Medallion in hand."

"Umm, no. But what I have to share with you will be a shock."

"Really? I can't think of anything else that you could tell me that would surprise me more than the Medallion is out of the chest," Cavelan chuckled.

"Well, I think this tops it," Gateskin replied with a wide grin.

Cavelan waited, holding his breath.

"We just had a delivery of two dragonets! Madrigal and Izara are new parents!"

"What? Are you kidding me, Gateskin? Do you mean you now have four dragons on Sovorotskina?"

"Yes!"

"That is truly unbelievable! When can I see them?"

"Well, that may be a while. I need to train them along with their parents' assistance. They are like little children and will be mischievous and out of control."

"I see. Are they dangerous to you and your family and villagers?"

"They could be, if left unattended."

"Oh no, I guess I will wait to see them. I don't want to be a meal for them."

"Haha, I don't think you have to worry about that. In fact, they have already learned one thing."

"Already? What is that?"

"They learned how to bow to Solinara and me." Gateskin answered, proudly.

"That is good to hear. They need to know who to revere right away. That you are not to be eaten," Cavelan chuckled.

"Yes, that is a good thing. I just need to keep my curious children away until I think it is time for them to meet."

"I know how that is. I could never keep mine away if I had dragons, never mind dragonets."

"Well, now stay on line while I open up a window for the rest of the rulers. This should be interesting," Gateskin instructed.

"I can't wait to see their expressions of envy, especially King Kaposkaran. He will be livid. He wasn't happy that you had two dragons. Now you have four!"

The windows opened in each of the neighboring villages with a ruler in each looking surprised to see Gateskin summoning them. Only one window was empty – King Kaposkaran as usual did not respond.

"Maybe we should wait a minute or two more for Parotovina to respond," Gateskin announced.

"What is it, Gateskin? You look like you have won some big prize. Is it the Medallion?" King Noderan of Amora asked.

"No, that is not what I wanted to share with you. That will happen another time, I'm sure."

The Healers of Merona asked, "Is this a positive thing, Gateskin, or should we be worried about something?"

"Just look at his face, Healers. He doesn't look like he is concerned about anything. In fact, he looks like a new father," King Zuri of Merlina exclaimed.

This remark caused Gateskin to smirk. Everyone looked at him and smiled.

"Are you going to be a new father, Gateskin?" King Kaposkaran asked as he opened his window after hearing the last words from Zuri.

"It's funny that you say that, Zuri. Nice of you to stop in, Kaposkaran. Both of you are wrong. It is not that at all."

"Well, when are you going to tell us, Gateskin?" Kaposkaran asked in his usual impatient manner.

"I have the most surprising news ever, men. My two dragons, Madrigal and Izara, just became parents of two dragonets."

"What are you saying?" Kaposkaran shouted.

"Are you kidding us, Gateskin?" The Healers queried.

"How can that be?" Zuri asked, frowning.

"I don't understand," King Noderan of Amora, interjected.

"Well, gentlemen. We all know how but it's the why that is the question. I guess you could say that they are healthy and well-fed dragons making for anything being possible."

"What are you going to do with four dragons, Gateskin?" Noderan asked.

"I plan to train the dragonets like I did their parents. If you are fearful of them, I can assure you that they will not harm anyone unless I say so."

"What does that mean, Gateskin?" Kaposkaran stressed in anger. "Are you going to send them to my land to murder me and my people?"

"Of course not, Kaposkaran. I would never do that. I will use them to keep my land safe and instruct them to guard the borders to keep out others who try to invade my village and harm my people."

Kaposkaran gave a humph sound before turning away from the window.

"I guess he is not going to listen to what I have to say next," Gateskin guffawed.

"I don't want any of you to fear these dragons. If you do not threaten me or my people, then you have nothing to fear. They will be our protectors against any harm coming to my land. If you want to visit, you must first contact me and I will meet you at the borders of our lands. You must not enter unannounced or you could be in danger."

"What?" King Zuri said with a grumble.

"I don't want you to feel unwelcome at all. I will be happy to have you visit only when I say it is safe. I need to train these dragons for a couple of months, maybe more. It took a while to train their parents but it may take longer to train these little ones. Just think how long it took you to train your children to behave."

The leaders nodded at Gateskin's words, except Kaposkaran who refused to meet anyone's eyes when he appeared in the window again. He was clearly upset.

"I guess that is all. I will let you know when it is safe to visit and meet these dragons. Thank you for taking the time to respond to my call. I promise to keep you informed about their progress. Oh, I almost forgot to tell you. The dragonets already know how to bow to my wife and me."

"Is that so? Wow, that is fantastic! Aren't we proud of you!" Kaposkaran said with deep anger and sarcasm.

Gateskin shook his head at Kaposkaran's sarcastic tone and said, "Well, it is time for me to close out. Thank you for listening. At least some of you listened well."

"Thank you, Gateskin, for sharing this wonderful news," Cavelan said as he looked at the others to respond.

"Yes, thank you for sharing this happy news," Noderan stated.

"I agree, it was a surprise, even a shock to hear, but we are happy for you," The Healers responded.

“Yes, we are pleased to hear this news and look forward to hearing more about these dragonets and when we can meet them,” Zuri added.

“What about you, Kaposkaran?” Cavelan asked.

There was no answer as the window into Parotovina darkened after Kaposkaran closed it.

All the other rulers closed their windows except for Cavelan who stayed to converse more with Gateskin. He was truly excited about this wonderful news and wanted to know everything about these dragonets. Gateskin was happy to comply, feeling like a new father himself. He shared what the new dragons looked like and how he thought that the male dragonet was going to be a handful.

# CHAPTER SIXTEEN

Madrigal woke up from his nap to his dragonets pulling on his ears. He quickly pushed them aside and pulled their ears to calm them down. This they didn't like but they calmed down once they saw their father's fiery eyes looking back at them.

Izara giggled at the sight of her mate and their offspring playing a tug of war with each other's ears.

"Izara, you should be training them not to do this to me," Madrigal exclaimed, feeling perturbed.

"You better get used to them. This is only the beginning. We need to train them not to do a lot of things. Look what they did while you were sleeping." She pointed to the mess at the back of the lair.

"What did they do? Oh no!! They defecated inside? We need to take them outside right now. They need to learn how to do their messy business outside." Madrigal huffed in anger and grabbed both dragonets by their ears and pulled them outside.

The dragonets shrieked out loud at being dragged outside. Once they were there, they tried to fly away but were not adept at doing that just yet. Their wings were not strong enough to hold them up.

Sunniva settled down and became more docile than her brother who continued to fight his father's efforts to train him to do his messes outside.

"Listen, Lorcan. I am your father and your master. You will obey me and listen to my words. I want you to pay close attention to everything that I tell you. This is important. When King Gateskin comes back you will listen to him also. He will be instructing both of you to become better dragons as he did for your mother and me. We are strong and are able to do amazing things. You must listen and learn. Don't you want to be all that you can be?"

"Yes, Father. I will listen," Lorcan responded with his head lowered so as not to meet his father's fiery eyes.

"What about you, Sunniva? Are you ready to listen and learn?"

"Yes, Father. I am ready," Sunniva said with a bow which brought a smile to Madrigal's face.

Izara waited at the doors of the lair. She smiled as she listened to her mate instruct their offspring. She felt such warmth and love for all of her family.

Madrigal caught his mate's eyes and sent a warm smile full of love back to her.

The two dragonets wandered a little further away as instructed by their father to do their business and return to him for further instructions.

Madrigal kept his eyes glued to them until they were back at his side. He nodded to them and pushed them along until they returned to the lair.

King Gateskin was hovering above watching this interchange with the new dragonets and their father. He chuckled to himself and then flew down announcing his presence as he did so.

"Ah, Madrigal. I see you are busy teaching your young ones to do…um…their business."

"Hello, King. Yes, they seem to think that they can do their business anywhere they choose. We have to nip that right away! It is already beginning to smell inside our lair from what they already did," Madrigal sighed.

"Don't worry about that. I will have the Queen come with some potions to clear out the stuff and the smell. She does wonders with such things. We have to deal with the wolves and other animals around who leave their messes outside our home or close to it."

"Oh, that isn't a good thing. I guess you can't train a wolf like you can a dragon or another animal."

"Well, we are working on that. Cantor, the leader is trying to instruct his offspring as you are doing. The only problem with that is he has too many offspring to teach."

"What are you going to do with all those wolves?" Madrigal asked.

"We are working on that issue at the moment. We may have to move some of them to other huts."

"What is their purpose here, King? I'm sorry if I am being impertinent asking this question."

"No, not at all, Madrigal. You are a citizen of Sovorotskina and have rights like anyone else and can ask any questions you have for me. As for the wolves, they guard the borders close to my home deterring anything from entering, especially the Catlings."

Madrigal bowed to the King and sighed in surprise. "I can see how important they are to the safety of the village. Also, thank you, kind ruler. I never expected you to extend such kindness to me. I thought I was in trouble for asking such an impertinent question."

"No, I would never punish you for asking anything, Madrigal. I respect you as you respect me."

"Yes, King. I do respect you and so will my dragonets very soon. I already told them that they will listen to me as their father and master as well as listen to you as their king and master."

"Very good to hear, Madrigal. I am proud of what you have become since you arrived here. You are an impressive and formidable dragon. I am most pleased to call you and Izara my dragons and citizens of Sovorotskina. I'm sure that I will feel the same about Lorcan and Sunniva soon."

"I will do my best to assure that you feel that way about them too. Sunniva is such a sweet dragonet but her brother is another matter. He may give us a little more trouble and fight us at every lesson."

"Do you remember when you first arrived here? Both of you were not as pleased with your new home, if you know what I mean."

"Ah, yes. I remember clearly. I was a little more receptive though. I guess Lorcan takes after his mother while Sunniva has my sweet personality," Madrigal laughed out loud at his own words.

His laughter soon dissipated as his mate called out to him, "What did you say, Madrigal?"

"Oops, I guess I may be in trouble, King Gateskin. I better soothe her temper before she gives me more grief. I love her but she can be trying at times."

"I can understand that. I have a wonderful mate too who also can be trying at times. But I love her in spite of that," Gateskin nodded and smiled as he turned to leave the dragons to their conversation.

Gateskin only hoped that Solinara wasn't listening in on his conversation with Madrigal.

Madrigal turned to Gateskin and called out, "King Gateskin? Wait a minute please. I need to share something with you."

Gateskin flew back down next to Madrigal and waited to hear what he had to say.

"I almost forgot to tell you something strange that happened as our eggs were hatching."

"What is that?"

"Well, I was thoroughly engrossed with the progress of the hatching, as you can imagine, when I felt a wind come around me from above."

"A wind?"

"Yes, I felt as if someone or something was watching the hatching over my shoulder. It was a little unnerving since I didn't see anything there. I didn't tell Izara or she would have been quite upset. She may have struck out at the wind."

"What do you think caused the wind, Madrigal?"

"I hesitate to say. That depends on who is capable of becoming invisible. Did you not tell me that Botular can do this?"

"Yes, I may have shared that with you. That is why he was under lock and key until the eggs were hatched."

"Oh, then it couldn't have been him. But who could have done that?"

"I will find out, don't worry about it, Madrigal. Have you noticed this wind again since the eggs hatched?"

"No."

"That's good. Take care of your mate and dragonets and let me worry about this wind. Okay?"

"Yes, of course, King. I have plenty to keep me occupied so that I don't worry."

"Good to hear. I will be back again soon with Queen Solinara when it is feeding time."

"Sounds good to me. I know we will all be hungry for her delicious food."

Gateskin nodded and flew back to his home. He had some investigating to do.

# CHAPTER SEVENTEEN

Gateskin found his wife in her workshop working on producing more food from her potions and spells with extra nutrition in each pail for the new dragonets.

Solinara looked up when she felt her husband's presence. "Hello, dear. Are the dragonets doing well? I hope they are not too hungry yet. I am almost finished with the new batch of food for them and their parents."

"I did tell Madrigal that you would be coming soon with the food. Also, the dragonets defecated inside the lair and you will need to bring some potions or whatever to clean it out of the droppings and the smell."

"Of course. I can do that. I will bring a potion along shortly before they eat to rid the smell and dissolve the detritus from the lair. Now what is bothering you, Gateskin. I can always tell by the look on your face and the deep crevice in your forehead between your brows."

"I guess I can't hide my problems from you, can I, sweetheart?"

"No, you cannot. Now, spill it. Tell me what is bothering you. Is it something to do with the dragons?"

"Well, maybe a little."

Solinara mixed up the food and set it aside as she waited for her husband to continue.

"Madrigal just shared something with me. He said when the eggs were hatching, he felt a wind above his head. It was like someone or something was there watching the eggs hatch over his shoulder even though he couldn't see anything there."

"Really? What or who do you think it was? Are you thinking about Botular?"

"I did right away, but he was locked up all that time."

"Okay, then who could have done that?"

"I think I may know of one person who is capable of disappearing like that."

"Oh no! You can't be serious, Gateskin! It can't be!"

"I think it was. One way to find out is to ask her."

"I am coming with you. She may be in the garden. I sent the three to fetch some vegetables for dinner."

Gateskin and Solinara flew over to the garden in a hurry to find out the truth. When they arrived, they settled down at the opposite end of the garden from their children who looked up in surprise.

"Hi Father and Mother. Do you need us for anything?" Serena asked.

"Yes, we need to speak with you three about something of utmost urgency."

"What?" Catalina said with eyes full of fear as she looked at her brother.

Simon laid his hand on his sister's arm to settle her down.

"What is it, Father?" Serena questioned with a frown of concern.

"Let's go back to the house and sit down. This may take a while to settle."

"Yes, Father," Serena answered, pushing her siblings along as they were shaking their heads and mumbling to themselves as they carried a basket full of vegetables.

Gateskin cleared his mind so that Serena couldn't read his thoughts and Solinara did the same.

Once they were all seated at the kitchen table, Gateskin began to question them.

"So, is there something that anyone would like to share with us?"

The siblings hung their heads and sighed heavily.

Gateskin and Solinara waited a few minutes for them to organize their thoughts and then stated, "I visited with the dragons a short time ago. Do you want to know what Madrigal told me?"

"What did he tell you, Father?" Catalina couldn't help asking.

"Well, he said that he felt a wind over his shoulder inside the lair as the eggs were hatching. What do you think about that? Who do you think could have done that?"

Gateskin looked from one child to the other waiting for a response. Solinara smiled weakly at her children and nodded for them to explain.

Serena began, "I…" but was interrupted by Catalina.

"No, Serena. I will explain. After all, it is my fault. You were not involved at all. I shouldn't have asked you to keep our secret."

Gateskin looked kindly on his youngest child and said, "Please go on, Catalina."

"I…I really wanted to see the eggs when they hatched, Father and Mother. I am so sorry. I convinced Simon to come with me so we could be the first ones to see the dragonets. I didn't want to cause any trouble. I hope Madrigal and Izara will not be angry with me." She sniffled and rubbed the tears away as they fell onto her hands.

"Catalina, sweetie. I can understand why you wanted to do that but it was a dangerous thing to do. Madrigal told me that only he felt the wind you caused being there. Luckily it wasn't Izara who felt your presence. Do you know what she would have done if she had?"

"No, Father," Catalina said with another sniffle.

"Madrigal told me that he purposely did not tell her for she would have brushed the wind away with her wings or possibly breathed fire on you."

"Oh no! We could have been killed, Father!" Simon announced in horror.

"Yes, that is correct, son. You would not be here to share this with us. Now do you understand how dangerous it is to do anything like that near the dragons without our permission and that of the dragons."

Catalina sighed, wiped her eyes and nose with a handkerchief her mother had handed her and said, "Yes, Father. I understand. I will never do that again!"

"Good! Now it is time for you three to visit the dragonets as long as you keep your distance and do everything I tell you. These creatures are dangerous. Do you understand?"

The three nodded back at their father, eyes wide with excitement and anticipation.

Solinara giggled at the sight of her children's enthusiasm. She also sighed in relief as she looked at her husband who nodded back. They shared the same relief in their minds that nothing had happened to their children for doing such a dangerous thing.

# CHAPTER EIGHTEEN

Gateskin spoke to Solinara in her head as they flew with their children to the dragons' lair. "Do you think I should share this with Madrigal about the children being the ones to witness the hatching?"

"No, I don't think so, dear. Madrigal may share this with Izara and she will not trust our children ever again. I think it is best forgotten by all to be on the safe side. Don't you agree?"

"Yes, I do. You are one brilliant wife. You always know the answer to tough questions. That is why I need your counsel daily." Gateskin winked at her and smiled.

The children were behind them and whispered together. "What do you think they are saying now, Serena?"

Serena shook her head. "I cannot read their minds. They have hidden their thoughts from me now. I am better off not knowing what they are thinking. It's safer for all of us."

"I guess. But maybe they are thinking up some punishment for us," Catalina whispered.

"Well then I think we better behave ourselves, Catalina," Simon added.

"Good idea, Simon. That was a smart thing to say. I hope you both remember that next time you want to do something crazy like that. Please don't include me," Serena stated with a stern look.

When they arrived at the lair, Gateskin announced their arrival and met Madrigal at the doorway of the lair. The dragon smiled up at them and welcomed them inside.

The children stayed behind their parents as they were directed for safety and peeked around them to see the dragonets sleeping peacefully with snores that seemed to blend in together and almost harmonize.

Izara bowed to the King and Queen and smiled at the children. She said, "My little ones will be waking soon to eat once again. Did you bring more food?"

Queen Solinara whipped the bag of food out of thin air and settled it down next to Izara so she could feed her dragonets when they woke.

"How are they doing, Izara?" Solinara asked.

"Surprisingly well, Queen Solinara. They have been much better about doing their business outside in the bushes away from the lair. The smell is better now after you left the potion in that spot when you last brought their food. We thank you for that. It was difficult to sleep with that smell permeating our senses."

"I can imagine that, Izara. We have issues with the wolves because of their numbers. I am working on that to keep their feces in an area away from our house and allow it to disintegrate quicker and dispel the odor."

"You do have your hands full, Queen. I hope we are not more of a burden to you."

"Not at all, Izara. It is a pleasure to do whatever I need to do to make you all feel at home. This is, after all, your new home and the only home your offspring have ever known."

"Yes, I hadn't thought of that. They don't know anything about our home of birth, Dragonaria. I guess we will have to share all that with them one day and explain how we arrived here."

“Yes, I guess you will have to do that.” Solinara turned to look at Gateskin for his thoughts on what Izara had just said.

He told her in her mind, “Don’t worry about that now. We will discuss this more at home.”

Solinara nodded in agreement and sighed as she watched the colorful and magnificent dragonets as their bodies rose and fell with their breathing. She hoped they would awaken soon so the children could see them in all their glorious splendor.

The children were speechless as they watched the dragonets in awe. They waited patiently for them to awaken.

Soon the dragonets started stretching and moaning as they woke up and looked around them to see five new faces in front of them. The faces that intrigued them more were the three smaller faces of the children who looked back at them and smiled.

“Oh, they are awake,” Izara announced.

"Let's bring them outside to do their business first, Madrigal. "Would you do the honors, dear?" Izara asked.

Madrigal pulled them up by their ears and dragged them out of the lair. They knew the drill now and went to their usual spot in the bushes to relieve themselves. After finishing and covering up their messes with dirt as their father had taught them, they looked back at the children who were watching them with their mouths open and eyes wide.

Sunniva ventured to move a little closer to the smallest child. "Hello," she said to Catalina who looked back at her unable to respond.

"Catalina, please say hello back to Sunniva," Solinara stated as she pushed her daughter forward.

"Hello, Sunniva. Nice to meet you."

Sunniva smiled showing her teeth which made Catalina back away and hide behind her mother.

"Please do not be frightened, Catalina," Madrigal announced as he stood beside Sunniva and petted her on her head. Sunniva sighed in pleasure and looked up at her father with love.

"See, she is not going to hurt you. I told her about your father and mother but did not share anything about the three of you. Now is the time to introduce yourselves to my dragonets. They are curious just like children are."

Simon stepped forward to show how brave he could be and introduced himself to Sunniva.

Sunniva bowed to him and smiled a little smaller so as not to frighten him like she had done to Catalina.

Lorcan stepped next to his sister and said, "Hi, I am Lorcan. I am the stronger one and fiercer than my sister but I won't eat you."

"Lorcan! Behave yourself," his mother scolded.

"Sorry. I thought it was a good idea to say that so they would not be afraid to come closer."

"I don't think that is funny, Lorcan." Sunniva stated as she pushed her brother aside.

Serena stepped forward now and announced her name and that she was the oldest. "I am pleased to meet you both, Sunniva and Lorcan. Right? I wasn't sure if I got the names right. Father shared them with us after your hatching."

"Yes, you got our names correct, Serena. It is a pleasure to meet you and your siblings too. We can be friends and grow up together," Sunniva said with a bounce of her wings to show her enthusiasm.

"Well, I think it is time for us to leave so that you can feed them," Gateskin and Solinara announced as they pushed their children along and waved goodbye to the dragons.

Catalina smiled back at Sunniva and waved happily at her. Sunniva winked and waved before going back inside the lair with Lorcan close behind. He waved to Simon and sighed, "He would have tasted very good though."

“What did you say, Lorcan?” his father asked him sternly.

“Umm…nothing, Father. I was just thinking out loud how nice it was to meet the King and Queen and their family.

“Hmm. I see.” Madrigal kept his eyes on Lorcan.

# CHAPTER NINETEEN

Solinara wanted to discuss what Izara had mentioned about teaching her offspring about Dragonaria.

"I understand your reluctance to consider this, dear. But it is not for us to decide what parents should teach their children. You would want your own children to know about where you grew up if it wasn't here. Right?"

"Hmm, I guess so, Gateskin. But I fear that the dragonets may want to leave here and go to Dragonaria to live."

"They may want to do that one day though. We can't stop them from living their lives if that is what they want to do."

"I don't want to think about losing them to that island, not yet. They are too young and need to mature."

"There is nothing wrong with Dragonaria and its rulers. King Marcellus and Queen Isla are good people. Their girls are…well, at least two of their girls are kind, not so much the oldest one."

"But what…"

"No more about this. We need not worry yet. We have to keep their birth a secret until I share this news with King Marcellus. It would be a good idea to do this soon, better than having him find out from someone else."

"Then he will want to come here to see them. What if he wants to take them back?" Solinara stressed.

"Yes, I believe he will. We have already discussed this, Solinara. Please, dear. Let me do the worrying. Okay? I need to check on Arubane and the Wizards and the chest. They are having difficulty with it."

"I hope Arubane is not still receiving the messages."

"That is why I need to see him and then the Wizards."

What's going on with the chest? You hadn't mentioned that, Gateskin."

"I know. This just happened. Let me explain." He continued to explain about how Arubane was receiving messages from the chest and that the four Wizards were having a difficult time containing the beams in the chest. They were unable to open it for fear of the beams escaping and causing harm to anyone as they had done in the past.

"Oh no! I'm sorry I am keeping you. Please go take care of that right away. We will discuss all this later. I need to create some more potions and prepare more food. These dragonets eat more than I thought they would. If you need me, let me know, Gateskin."

Gateskin nodded, kissed his wife softly on the lips and hugged her. He didn't want her to feel as if he were dismissing her concerns. He hadn't wanted to admit that he was feeling the same concerns about the dragonets.

After Gateskin left, Solinara thought of how she would prepare the food for all the animals and repeat the process using a little of her powers. She couldn't spend half her life with food preparation like this. She gathered all her herbs, greens, flower petals, small animals that she had caught and slain, and mixed all together with her potions. When she had made enough, she used her potions to copy each bag repeatedly until she had filled one end of her workshop with enough to last a month at a time, some for the barn animals, wolves and dragons. She would keep doing this until she had enough to last a year. A potion waved over the lot would keep the food fresh indefinitely. She sighed and left her workshop to attend to other matters.

While Solinara was working her magic, Gateskin flew over to Hotenfaran and Procelina's home to check on Arubane.

Hotenfaran met him at his front door and welcomed the King in. "I was hoping that you would return soon. I am concerned about Arubane. He was delirious and repeating something over and over again."

"What is he saying?"

"Now is the time to collect your prize. You must not hesitate. Do it now!"

"Is he saying what he is supposed to collect?"

"No. But maybe he is lucid now. We let him rest for a while. Procelina gave him a potion to sleep.

He was exhausted from all this feedback he was receiving."

"He was quite upset when I saw him. That is why I brought him back to you. I think it is the chest and what is inside it – the Medallion and whatever else the wizard put in there many years ago."

"Do you think it could have been a distant relative of Arubane's? Maybe a grandfather or great grandfather?"

"That is quite possible. It was long ago. Too long ago for it to be his parents. Besides they died before they could share any of their genealogy with him. Besides, he was too young to explain all that then."

"I agree, Gateskin. We don't know anything other than he was born in Parotovina and escaped under the guise of a black sheep among the white sheep. That is how we found him. I still remember so clearly how he turned back into a boy of five years old right in front of us. If I hadn't seen that with my own eyes, I would never have believed that such a young child could do something so complex. I can't even do that as a wizard myself. Can you, Gateskin?"

"I don't know if I could. I have never tried. But I know that I couldn't have done that at such a young age."

"Right. I know better than to ask you that. You are the most powerful of wizards anywhere in Noella Province."

"Maybe or maybe not."

"What do you mean?"

"Well, do you remember what I said to Arubane when you brought him here?"

"Remind me, please, Gateskin."

"I told Arubane that he was so powerful that I would want him as my own personal wizard one day when he grew up."

"Oh, I remember now. I thought you were just being a kind uncle."

"No, I meant it and I mean it even more now. If he has the powers of that wizard who buried the chest, then he can do just about anything."

"Really? Well, I know he has done a lot of unusual things around here. He built the barn/workshop over there where he prepares potions and all kinds of unusual things to help us farm this land. He is one extremely talented young man. He is almost a man now or at least he acts much older than he is. Have you noticed how tall he is now, almost taller than I am at over six feet. It feels as if he is getting older faster than normal."

"Are you concerned about this, Hotenfaran?"

"Well, yes, I am. So is Procelina. She keeps saying that it appears he has grown another inch a week."

"Hmm. Why haven't you mentioned this to me sooner?"

"You have so much to do on this land and so many things to handle. You don't need my problems on top of all that."

"Hotenfaran, you are family. Don't ever forget that. I know I haven't talked to you lately because of the dragons and other things but I am always here for you if you need me and so is your sister."

"Yes, of course. I realize that. Maybe we should visit Solinara one day and have tea. We can discuss all of this and decide what we must do. I am more concerned now than ever with these messages he is receiving. What are we to do about it, Gateskin?"

"Please get in touch with your sister and meet with her. She is an intelligent and powerful fairy who can help you maybe more than I can. I value her counsel daily."

"Okay, Procelina and I will do that and bring Arubane along. I want her to see him for herself how grown up he has become in a short span of time."

"Good. Now I need to see Arubane and maybe decipher more about this message from him. I know that the chest is the thing that is sending the messages but that is all I know."

Arubane was sitting at the edge of his bed with his mother by his side watching him eat a sandwich. He perked up once he saw Gateskin.

Gateskin smiled at Arubane and asked, "How are you feeling?"

Arubane shrugged his shoulders and kept eating his sandwich.

Gateskin turned to Procelina, "Hello, Procelina. Good to see you."

"Nice to see you too, Gateskin. We are relieved you are here to take care of our Arubane. We are deeply worried."

"Yes, I am here. Please don't worry. All will be good and work out. I promise you." Gateskin leaned in and gave his sister-in-law a hug before she left the room.

"Oh, Uncle, it is good to see you again. I was worried that you forgot all about me. I'm sorry if I caused you any concern," Arubane said with a sigh of relief.

"Not at all, Arubane. I wanted to see how you are feeling now. Have the messages stopped?"

"Yes, they did once I was sleeping. Now I only hear a whisper. Do you think it is coming from the chest?"

"Yes, it definitely is. It is trying to tell you something about what is inside. We think it contains the Medallion that was buried one hundred years ago by a wizard who visited the area. He was trying to hide it from another wizard. That is what we have heard over the years. Many others tried to find the Medallion until we discovered the chest buried in the Ailylene Mountain in Sovorotskina with the help of the dragons."

"Yes, I remember that. But why is it trying to contact me now? I never heard anything after it was uncovered. Why did it wait until now to begin messaging me?"

"That is a good question, Arubane. Evidently it was waiting for you to grow up. Speaking of that, I noticed you have grown several inches and appear to be much older suddenly. Do you feel any different?"

"Yes, I do, Uncle Gateskin. I have muscles and more hair everywhere that I didn't have just last year. Why is that? Why is this happening to me?"

"Please do not worry, Arubane. Some children grow faster and go through a stage before they are a man. That is what is happening to you. You are becoming a man sooner than others your age."

"But I don't like it. I want to be a boy longer."

"I understand. I will be by your side though this time and make sure no harm comes to you. Okay?"

"Okay. I feel stronger when you are near me. I don't understand it, but I do. Maybe I need your powers to protect me from…."

"From what, Arubane?"

"I feel an evil presence. That is what I don't like. I think it is trying to take over my mind."

"Why do you say that, Arubane?"

"Well, besides the messages from the chest, I also hear another message coming through."

"What is the message?"

"It is saying that I must find it and bring it to him."

"Bring the chest to someone?"

"Yes, I think that is what it means."

Gateskin didn't say another word but ran his hands over Arubane's head to interfere with whatever was trying to enter his mind. He feared it was something more than just the chest. He would find a way to stop it before it destroyed this boy who was now a young man still aging.

# CHAPTER TWENTY

Gateskin left Arubane after he fell asleep, with the King's help, to meet with the boy's parents. Hotenfaran was sitting at the kitchen table with his wife sipping tea and looking stressed.

The parents jumped up when they saw Gateskin coming toward them.

"Arubane is sleeping now. I put him to sleep so that his mind will not be tasked. He needs to rest."

"Thank you, Gateskin. Yes, he does need to rest and rid those messages from reaching him," Procelina exclaimed as she hung her head in her hands with tears raining down.

"I will be close by if you need me again. Let me know how he feels when he wakes again."

"We will. What can we do to stop this from happening to him?" Hotenfaran asked.

"I will work on that and let you know. Solinara will have a potion to help him rest. I will have her stop by. In the meantime, I will be working on a way to stop these messages completely. Did he tell you about the other messages he is receiving now?"

"Other messages? He is receiving other messages besides the ones from the chest?"

"Yes, he shared that with me now. He feels it is evil that is trying to take over his mind."

"What are the messages?" Procelina queried with a deep frown.

Gateskin explained, "Someone is telling him, 'Take it and bring it to me?' Meaning most likely, the chest."

"Is there an evil wizard out there who is a descendant of the one who was searching for the Medallion after it was buried by the other wizard?"

"It looks that way, Hotenfaran. I suspect that is the case. I don't like that we have to deal with this evil one trying to take over control of Arubane's mind."

"Oh no! It can't be happening to our son!" Procelina cried out. "You must stop it, Gateskin. You've got to save our boy. He shouldn't be a man already. It is too soon. He is just a boy."

"I agree. This shouldn't be happening to him. I will do all in my power to stop it even if I have to destroy the chest to do it."

"Maybe that is the only way to protect Arubane," Hotenfaran agreed.

Procelina looked up with a tear-stained face and nodded. She hugged her husband and sighed through more tears.

Gateskin sent positive thoughts to Hotenfaran and Procelina and left. He planned to speak with the Wizards again and see how the chest was behaving.

The Wizards were putting more spells on the chest to keep it contained as Gateskin came to their door.

The King motioned for them to sit down so he could explain what was happening to Arubane and what he thought they could do to stop this.

The Wizards listened and nodded. "This does sound like the chest is trying to control the boy and the descendant of the evil wizard is trying to take over the chest and its powerful artifacts," Marno stated in a firm tone.

"Yes, I agree," Fortag, Wassor and Tornak exclaimed in unison.

"This is a sad day for a young boy to have to deal with something like this. He should not be forced to be a man. He isn't ready," Tornak said in a voice that was full of distress.

"I know. Arubane is quite upset. He isn't ready to be a man. He is only a boy and should be able to enjoy being a boy until he is ready to be a man," Gateskin asserted.

"Something is making him older than he should be so that he can handle what is coming," Wassor stated with a frown.

"I agree. Something is coming this way and Arubane will be in the middle of it. He is not ready for whatever this is," Gateskin stressed.

"What can we do, King? Should we destroy the…" before Marno could finish his sentence, the chest inside the vault banged against the door.

"What caused that?" Tornak asked.

"It is what I almost said, Tornak. It heard us speaking of it and did not like what we were saying," Wassor explained.

"Yes, I do believe it can hear us," Marno asserted.

"We need to move away from here. Come with me, Wizards. We need to discuss this more," Gateskin announced almost in a whisper.

The four Wizards followed the King out of their house and down the road to Gateskin's home. He led the Wizards to his Conference Room where he closed off the door and the room became sound-proof. He sent word to his wife to join them as soon as she could.

Solinara came a few minutes later and sat at the table with the men. She had received a quick summary from Gateskin as she headed over from her workshop.

"We are all concerned for the welfare of this poor boy who is becoming a man before his time. These messages will and can destroy him if he completes the task that the wizard from long ago planned. The wizard who buried this chest wanted to keep it from the other wizard who had evil intentions to use its powers to destroy others and maybe our lands too. The first wizard was a kind one and didn't think that anyone would ever uncover it. It was a sad day when we did that. If we had only known what danger it would cause, we would have left it alone," Gateskin explained sadly.

"What will you do, Gateskin?" Solinara asked, knowing full well what that would be.

"I will destroy the chest and whatever else is in it. This may be the only way to save Arubane. It will kill him if we don't. Do you all agree?"

Marno exchanged looks with his fellow Wizards and nodded. "Yes, we agree. We cannot control it and it is only doing more damage each day we keep it."

"If we destroy it, King, then what?" Fortag asked.

"Well, it will stop sending messages for one thing and cease to have control over Arubane. He will then revert back to being a boy again."

"But how will we destroy it?" Wassor questioned.

"We will find a way. We must first put a spell over it so that it cannot stop us from touching it."

"What kind of spell, King?" Tornak queried.

"That is for all of you to create. I will add my own powers to it to bind it. Now you must get to work. You cannot do that in your home for it will know. You must stay here and work. I will keep this room contained away from my family and will make sure that you are fed and cared for during this time."

"Will we be able to leave here from time to time, King?" Wassor questioned.

"Of course. You will need to take breaks and then return to your work. I will be stopping in to see how you are doing."

"Good, we will work fast and come up with a spell that will contain it and then destroy it once and for all," Marno announced in a determined manner.

"Thank you, Wizards. I will be back shortly to check on things."

Solinara left the room with Gateskin. She needed to ask him more about Arubane. She went to the kitchen to prepare tea and some scones and little cakes for the Wizards then she would sit with her husband to discuss this further.

"How did Arubane look to you, Gateskin?"

"I am concerned, Solinara. He did not look good. He was aging before my very eyes. It was disturbing to see. His parents are quite distressed and will be coming to see you. I told them to stop by so you could see Arubane and judge for yourself. I know you have some powerful potions that will help him relax and may stop the age progression for a little while."

"Yes, I will work on them right away but first tell me what you plan to do."

"Once the Wizards have the spell powerful enough to put the chest at rest, then we will destroy it. I was planning on Madrigal helping me with that. I don't know if the chest can withstand fire for long. If it can, then I don't know what else to do." Gateskin sighed heavily.

"If you put a spell upon it then another spell, maybe then you can control it. Maybe you will be able to open it and take out whatever it is that is controlling these messages. It may be more than the Medallion," Solinara stated.

"You may be right there, dear. I will be adding my own spells to the Wizards' and then taking the chest back to the Ailylene Mountain to rebury it if I can't destroy it with fire."

"What if that other wizard, the evil one's descendant, returns and finds it? Will you be able to stop him from doing harm to all of us?"

"I will do all that is in my power to protect you and our family and village from this evil wizard. I haven't used all my powers yet, Solinara. I have not been using them to my full potential. I have much more to offer this land."

"Oh, I know you do. Sometimes you are holding back some of your powers so as not to harm anyone. But I know the powers of Gateskin are something no one can imagine, not even me," Solinara said with a grin.

"Well, we will see, won't we, Solinara," Gateskin grinned back at her but this grin did not reflect in his eyes.

# CHAPTER TWENTY-ONE

The three royal children were walking around their land staying away from the dragons per their parents' request. They passed by Botular's house and kept going until they came to Henno and Jennara out in their garden.

Henno and Jennara were formerly from Parotovina. They possess powers unlike other citizens of their village but they kept them quiet so as not to interest the King. If King Kaposkaran knew about their powers, he would have forced them to use them under his command. They managed to escape one day and fled to asylum in Sovorotskina where they now are secure and happy and use their powers only when the good King Gateskin requests their help.

The royal children waved to the couple and kept walking. They looked down into the village square and saw the villagers moving around as if they were worried about something.

"What are they doing, Serena?" Catalina asked.

"I don't know. They look like they are in a hurry."

"Should we go check on them?" Simon questioned as he met his older sister's eyes.

"No, I don't think it is our place to bother them. Let's go visit with Arubane and Uncle Hotenfaran and Aunt Procelina."

"Okay. We haven't seen them for a little while. They were traveling and were supposed to come visit us," Catalina announced. "Why didn't they come?"

"Let's find out," Simon added as they increased their steps to reach their relative's house.

Hotenfaran's and Procelina's house was situated close to Lake Serena where their uncle liked to fish. It was also helpful for Hotenfaran to keep an eye out for any stragglers who entered Sovorotskina. He acted as a scout for the King.

Spindle had been out surveying the border with Mitteran and noticed Serena and her siblings walking toward Arubane's house. He called down to them, "Where are you going?"

"Hi, Spindle," Serena answered as she felt her cheeks blushing a bright pink. She always did that when she saw Spindle. "We are going to visit our cousin, and aunt and uncle."

"I don't think you should do that right now. Arubane is sick."

"He is sick? What's wrong?" Serena asked with deep concern, edging her brows.

"I think you should speak with your father before you visit. He will explain," Spindle stated in a serious tone.

When Spindle was serious like that Serena knew something was definitely wrong. She nodded and turned her siblings around to return home right away. She needed to know what was going on and why they were not told about their cousin being sick.

Upon arriving home, Serena went inside first to find her father. She expected he was inside since she had looked all over the area surrounding their house.

When she entered, she saw her mother in the kitchen brewing tea and making scones and little tea cakes. Maybe Mother will share something about our cousin with me, she surmised.

"Mother, what is wrong with Arubane?"

Solinara did not turn to face her daughter but kept on placing scones and the little tea cakes on the grate of the wood stove.

"Mother, did you hear me?" Serena was getting antsy.

"Yes, I heard you, honey. Let me finish up with this batch and then we can sit and discuss this further.

Serena waited as patiently as she could, tapping her fingers on the table and keeping her eyes on her mother as she worked expertly and faster than the normal eyes could discern.

"That must be a record even for you, Mother," Serena chuckled.

"Well, maybe it is. I need to bring these into the Conference Room now. I will be right back. Sit tight. Have a scone and some tea while you wait."

Serena poured herself the tea and nibbled on a scone which was still warm, crispy on the outside and sweet and tangy on the inside. Her mother made the best scones and cakes in the province.

Solinara set the tea and scones and cakes on the table in front of Gateskin and the Wizards who stopped what they were doing to help themselves.

She whispered to Gateskin, "Serena is out in the kitchen asking about Arubane. Do you want me to explain what is going on or do you want to do that yourself?"

"No, I can't leave here now. Once the Wizards are finished cleaning up the plate of pastries, we will get right back to work. If she doesn't accept the explanation, then I will come out and explain in more detail. Just tell her that it is the chest that is causing him distress, nothing more for now. We are not quite sure what is happening ourselves but soon we will, I surmise."

"All right, but you know how insistent your eldest daughter is! She will want the whole truth and nothing less," Solinara winked at him, picked up the empty plate and whisked all the crumbs away with a little bit of magic.

The Wizards smacked their lips and said, "Thank you, Queen Solinara, for these magnificent scones and these sweet little cakes! No one can work magic in the kitchen like you can."

"You are most welcome. If you need anything else, please let me know." She moved out of the room without another word and hurried back to the kitchen where her daughter was still sipping her tea and looking off into the distance with a frown.

"All right, Serena. Here is the story. If you need more detail you will have to wait to see your father, per his request. He and the Wizards are working on this issue now as we speak."

“What issue, Mother? I was asking about Arubane. What is wrong with him that we can’t visit him? Is it something that is contagious?”

Solinara sighed and laced her hands together in front of her face as if she were in prayer. Serena watched her mother’s face for any signs of distress.

“Is Arubane going to die?” Serena’s voice was tight with emotion.

“Oh no, honey. I didn’t mean to make this sound so ominous. We are still working out the details of what is happening to him.”

“What is happening to him, Mother? Why are you talking in circles? This is very disconcerting. Please explain it to me. I am an intelligent teenager and understand big words.”

“I know you are, Serena. It is difficult to explain since we do not understand it yet ourselves.”

“Well, try me. Maybe I can come up with an explanation why he is sick or whatever.”

"We think that the chest and whatever is inside it is making Arubane…"

"What, Mother? Please continue. I can take the worse news since you already said he is not dying."

"Well, umm…"

"He is dying, isn't he? That is why you can't tell me!"

"No, it is not that. Well, it is difficult to understand what is happening even for your father and me. Let me try to go back a little in history."

"Oh, Mother. What are you trying to say? I have never seen you so inconsistent in your explanations. You always get right down to the facts. Please do so now."

"Okay. The chest was buried by a wizard, a kind one who did not want others to take possession of this chest and what was inside it because it could bestow great powers on whoever had it as long as they were a wizard. He buried it deep inside Ailylene Mountain. You know the rest of how it was found by your father and the dragons."

"Yes, I know all that. But what does this have to do with Arubane being sick?"

"I am getting to that. The chest has been sending messages to Arubane that are causing him to…get sick. Your father and the Wizards are working on some spells to contain the chest and the beams that are trying to escape. Your father wants to destroy it so the messages will no longer go to Arubane."

"But what are the messages and why are they making Arubane sick?"

"I think your father should try to explain the rest. For now, you must stay away from your aunt's and uncle's house until we fix this situation and destroy the chest. You must not share this with anyone. Do you understand?"

"Yes, mother, but I still don't understand what is happening to Arubane and why."

"We are puzzled by it all too. But remember this was a powerful wizard, not as powerful as your father but close to it, I'm sure. What he did was to protect others from something like this happening."

"It is all still a mystery to me, Mother. Your explanation did not tell me much about Arubane's health. I am worried. I don't want him to die."

"No, we don't either, honey. We are doing all we can to keep him healthy and safe. Just be patient. When this is completed, your father will tell you everything that you need to know."

"I hope so because I have an active imagination and can imagine the worst in a situation like this when it involves someone I love." Serena turned and left the kitchen to find her siblings who were playing with thc wolves' new pups. She knew that her siblings would want an explanation too which she didn't have."

Simon and Catalina looked up as their sister came toward them looking more distressed than before.

"What did Father say?" Simon asked.

"I didn't see Father but Mother told me some things which I don't understand because they do not explain anything about Arubane's health and why he is sick," Serena explained.

She continued to repeat everything that her mother had told her. She watched her siblings' faces and the confusion that was mirrored on their faces.

"That doesn't make any sense," Simon stated, frowning and shaking his head.

"I don't understand any of that either, Serena," Catalina interjected.

"I feel the same. But we are not to share this with anyone per Mother. We will get into trouble if we do. Remember that! You are already on the hot seat now for what you both did with the dragonets. You can't afford another problem. Father won't be so forgiving next time."

"I know but…," Catalina began.

"No buts, Catalina. I can see the wheels turning in your head. You are planning something again. We cannot do anything until Father and the Wizards fix this problem with the chest."

"I know but, please listen to me, Serena. I have an idea. Father and Mother don't have to know about this."

"Catalina, no, you will not go visit Arubane. That was Mother's orders. We need to stay away until this problem is solved and he is all better."

"How did you know I was going to suggest that we go visit while we're invisible?"

"Did you forget that I can read minds, Catalina?"

"Yes, I did. I forgot to clear my mind out before you could do that."

"Forget it completely and erase it out of your mind now. Maybe Mother will let us visit the dragons. Let me ask her. That will keep us busy."

"Okay, I guess," Catalina responded with a sigh as she looked at her brother for advice.

"No, I do not want to be part of your insane schemes. You already got me into trouble last time. Let's see if Mother will let us visit the dragonets."

"All right!" Catalina moaned and groaned as she sat down on the ground near the wolf pups so they could come onto her lap and cuddle.

Serena went back to see her mother.

# CHAPTER TWENTY-TWO

Serena returned quickly with a smile on her face as she met with her siblings who were playing with the wolf cubs.

"Well, it must be a positive thing since you are smiling now, Serena," Simon said, smiling back at her.

"Yes, it is," Simon.

Catalina just nodded glumly and kept patting the cubs and not meeting her sister's eyes.

"Well, are you going to listen to me, Catalina?"

"Yeah, I guess. Are we going to be able to visit the dragonets?"

"Yes, Mother said we could as long as we announce our presence and wait for the dragons to allow us to enter the lair. If they do not, then we need to return home right away and not go anywhere near Arubane's house."

"I know, we can't see Arubane yet. But when? I am even more really curious now that we know something is wrong with him," Catalina stressed with a deep-seated frown between her brows.

"Of course you are, little sister," Serena stated, hands on her hips, as she looked sternly at Catalina.

"Come on, Catalina. Let's go. I want to see the dragonets. They must be growing bigger every day," Simon urged, as he pulled his sister up from the ground.

Serena grabbed Catalina's hand as she and Simon flew their sister between them to the dragons' lair.

When they arrived, Serena called out to Madrigal, "Can we visit with you and your family today?"

Madrigal appeared at the immense doorway of the large lair and peeked his head out. "The King's family are always welcome here. Come in. You may have to wait a little while since the dragonets are taking another nap."

"That's okay. We just want to take a peek at them to see how much they have grown," Serena responded.

Simon and Catalina pushed their way past their sister who was trying to keep them at a safe distance from the sleeping dragonets.

"They are okay, Serena. My children will not wake up unless they smell some food."

"I hope they won't think we are food," Simon said with a look of horror on his face.

"No, not at all, Simon. They are not like that. I have trained them to only like the food that your mother, the Queen, brings them. I want them to get used to that only."

"Good idea, Madrigal," Simon stressed, relief flooding his face now.

"Haha. You are a funny young man, Simon," Madrigal chuckled.

Izara entered the lair to hear her mate's words. "What is so funny, Madrigal?"

"Simon is quite comical. He is worried that our offspring will think of him and his siblings as food."

Izara raised her scaly brows and said, "That is not too farfetched, dear."

"What?" Simon exclaimed.

"Not to worry, Simon. I promise you. You are safe here with me. If you entered alone then maybe you wouldn't be as safe. They are still young ones and need a lot of training."

"How come our father hasn't begun their training yet?" Catalina quizzed.

"Well, he has been busy elsewhere I imagine. He stopped by to tell me about this chest causing some problems with Arubane. Besides, I have been training them a little each day."

"That's good. Yes, we heard about Arubane being sick," Serena answered.

"It is a shame what is happening to Arubane though. I hope they can stop it soon."

"What is happening to him?" Catalina asked, her ears perking up to this news.

Madrigal looked up in alarm. "Didn't your parents tell you about that?"

"Not exactly. They told us Arubane was sick and that the chest was doing something to him," Catalina answered.

"Oh, I see. Well, it is up to them to explain more and not for me to say." Madrigal closed his mouth and looked away from them. He poked his children to wake them up in order to avoid the subject.

Sunniva looked up at her father and said, "Is it time to eat, Father? Is that why you woke me?"

"Not yet, Sunniva. You have visitors who want to see you."

"Oh, yes. Hello, children. It's so nice to see you again."

"You have grown so much since we last saw you, Sunniva," Simon stated, his eyes growing wider in awe at the beautiful dragon with yellow and turquoise scales that sparkled even in the dim light of the lair.

"Thank you, Simon. You are quite handsome yourself."

Simon blushed and looked away.

"Did I embarrass you, Simon. I am so sorry," Sunniva said, aghast.

Hearing his sister's voice, Lorcan opened his eyes and looked at the visitors. "Well, look who is here."

Serena nodded and smiled at Lorcan. "You are looking quite impressive with your gorgeous red and purple scales, Lorcan."

The dragonet was surprised by the eldest child's compliment. He hadn't expected that and was at first speechless.

"Umm, I…thank you, Serena. You are quite lovely yourself with your golden tresses."

Serena dipped her head and grinned at Lorcan. "You are most kind to say that, Lorcan."

"What about me? Don't I look good? I have golden hair too. Mine has more curls," Catalina announced with a pout.

"Of course, little one. You are the most beautiful young girl I have ever met," Lorcan bowed to her and winked at Serena and Simon who were hiding a giggle.

Madrigal and Izara exchanged grins in surprise at Lorcan's kindness to Catalina and Serena. It was out of character for him to act like that.

"I think you have a fan, Catalina. Lorcan never says anything nice like that. Also, you too, Serena. I think Lorcan likes beautiful girls," Madrigal stated with a chuckle.

"Why not?" Lorcan said with a wide grin.

"Do you want to go outside to play together?" Izara asked.

"Do you mean we can play with the dragonets?" Simon asked in surprise.

"Yes, as long as they are careful not to hurt you," Madrigal added as he looked at his offspring with a stern warning. “I will be keeping my eyes on you!”

“Of course, Father. We will be careful and not harm the children in any way,” Sunniva answered.

The children left the lair and followed the dragons to the wide spaces that surrounded the lair and ran through the high grass as the dragonets flew above them.

“You can fly now?” Serena asked in surprise.

“Yes, Father has been working with us to fly a little every day. We also practice when he is sleeping,” Lorcan bragged.

Sunniva nodded and grinned.

Serena flew up beside the dragonets and reached out to touch their wings. Simon soon joined her leaving Catalina below to cry out in protest.

“All right. We will bring you up here, Catalina,” Simon announced as he flew down and gripped his sister's hands and held on tight so she could also touch the dragonets' wings.

The dragonets bowed and gestured to the children to hop on their backs so that they could ride together.

"You want us to ride on you?" Serena asked in shock.

"Of course. Why not? If you slip you can always fly back up," Lorcan stated.

"Well, Simon and I can fly but not Catalina."

"Oh, I didn't know that. Sorry," Lorcan apologized.

"That's okay. I will hold on tight to your scales and not fall, I promise," Catalina stated in a thrilled voice.

"If you think you can, Catalina," Lorcan answered.

"She can ride on my back, Lorcan. I don't trust you to be careful," Sunniva stressed.

Catalina nodded and agreed, "Yes, I think I would be safer to ride with Sunniva."

Serena placed her sister securely on the female's back and sat behind her to ensure she was secure.

Simon hopped onto Lorcan's back and held on tight. Lorcan huffed in disagreement. He looked at his sister and frowned. "Why do you get the beautiful ones?"

"You have one, Lorcan. Stop complaining and enjoy the time we have with the King's children. This is an honor," Sunniva responded back with a frown.

"Hey, what's wrong with me?" Simon yelled out disconcerted.

The dragonets and children flew around and stayed close to the lair as instructed by their parents until Catalina whispered in Sunniva's ear.

# CHAPTER TWENTY-THREE

Gateskin looked up when he felt a wind blowing over him. What he saw did not please him one bit. He went inside his home to alert Solinara what he had seen.

Solinara raced out of the kitchen after finishing everything she was cooking with a wave of her hand and flew with Gateskin to the dragons' lair.

They discussed what they would do before they arrived. Landing outside the lair they called out to Madrigal and Izara, "We need to speak with you both right away."

Madrigal came outside first, followed closely by Izara. Madrigal responded when he saw the displeasure on their faces, "King and Queen, it is a pleasure to see you. Is there something wrong? You both look upset."

"Yes, we are quite upset. What are our children doing flying around on your dragonets? It is too soon and dangerous. They are not trained to handle any passengers."

"Oh, I didn't think of that. They were sure that they could do this and are doing a wonderful job of it. Don't you think so, King?" Madrigal grinned as he watched his dragonets with deep pride. But when he looked back at the King and

Queen, they were not evidencing any pleasure about what was taking place.

“You need to call them back right now, Madrigal,” Gateskin’s voice was filled with anger and disappointment.

“Yes, please call them back now, Madrigal,” the Queen requested with trepidation.

Izara responded, “I’m sorry, King and Queen if this displeases you. We thought that they were ready to do this. They have been practicing flying daily. We didn’t tell them to do it though. They did this on their own. They all look so happy and are having a wonderful time that we didn’t stop them.”

Solinara watched her children and relaxed when she noticed how happy they were, as Izara had stated.

She whispered to Gateskin, “I think they are doing quite well considering this is their first time flying on the dragonets.”

Gateskin assented, "Hmm, I see. They do need to be instructed not to veer too close to the borders of the other villages or over the UT."

"I agree, King Gateskin. I will instruct them on that right away. Let me call them back now. They have been up there long enough," Madrigal stated in a serious tone now, fearful that he was in trouble with the King.

When the children came closer to the lair, they noticed their parents and called out to them and waved.

Their parents did not wave back. Their faces showed disapproval and fear.

Serena whispered to her sister, "What did you say to Sunniva?"

"I told her to keep going forward but keep an eye out for anyone that may be out around the borders. I wanted to see how the UT looks from up here too. Maybe we can spot a Catling or two."

“Oh no, Catalina. I think we are in deep trouble. Look at Mother’s and Father’s faces. They don’t look happy. You better not say a word about what you told Sunniva to do. Luckily, she did not get that far.”

“I don’t plan to say a word. Not after seeing Father so angry. He looks as if he will explode any minute.”

“What are you two whispering about?” Simon wanted in on their secrets.

“We will tell you later. For now, we are in a lot of trouble as you can see by our parent’s faces,” Serena warned.

“I noticed. But what did we do to displease them?” Simon asked in confusion.

“It was nice while it lasted though,” Catalina sighed and hugged Sunniva’s neck and whispered, “Thanks.” Sunniva nodded and grinned showing all her teeth.

Simon leaned forward and did the same to Lorcan who just grunted his reply.

The villagers had spied the dragonets overhead and gathered in the square to observe them. They pointed at the colors that bounced off the dragonet's scales and the small people who were on their backs. They couldn't tell who these people were though since the dragonets flew so high.

"Do you think they are coming this way to introduce themselves to us?" Marion asked with a broad smile.

"I don't think so. Look, they are landing now. We can't see them anymore. The lair is too far away for us to spy on them. The King wanted it that way to keep us away and safe while they mature," Silas explained.

"Yes, I realize that, Silas, but I am still curious to see them up close. They are so beautiful. They created a rainbow effect in the sky with their gorgeous scales. I wonder which one is the female," Marion replied clearly in awe of them.

"We will know soon enough, people. Just be patient. King Gateskin assured me that when they are fully trained, they would come to introduce themselves along with their parents," Silas explained as he pushed the villagers back in the direction of their homes. He was wondering about all this himself as he headed back to his own home.

***

Back at the King's home, he and Solinara sent their children to his now empty Conference Room for a meeting since the Wizards had returned to their own place. There was much they would need to discuss with their children who seemed to think that they could do whatever they wanted with the dragonets without so much as a thought of how dangerous it was.

Serena looked at her parents and began, "We did not know that you did not want us to fly on the dragonets yet, Father and Mother. If we did this too soon, we all apologize and will not do it again until you say it is safe."

Their parents looked back at the three children and did not say a word but let them stew a while longer.

Catalina sighed and so did Simon while they waited to be scolded and punished for what they had done.

Several minutes passed and still no word from their parents who continued to look at them with frowns furrowing between their brows.

Finally, Catalina couldn't stand it for one more minute. "Well, are you going to say something to us, yell, reprimand, and punish us once and for all. We can't sit here all day like this, can we?" Her eyes were wide and full of concern.

"We are truly sorry. Is that what you want to hear from us?" Simon said in exasperation.

Catalina joined in, "I am sorry too, Father and Mother. We did not want to displease you. You did say we could go visit the dragons but didn't specify that we couldn't do anything with them."

Gateskin and Solinara stopped frowning and looking displeased at their children.

The King cleared his throat and stated, "Well, it looks like you did know that it would not be something we would approve of because of the danger it could be for all of you."

Solinara added, "Why did you do that? Did you not think about what could have happened if you had fallen off of the dragonets and landed somewhere in the UT or close to it?" The Queen shuddered as she said this.

Gateskin added, "The dragonets are still learning how to fly and not experienced yet having someone ride on their backs."

Serena exchanged looks with her siblings and they all nodded. "Yes, you are right, Mother and Father. We did not think. All we wanted to do was experience the thrill of flying on their backs without a concern for our safety. We are truly sorry that we did that."

"Well, it looks like you understand why we were so angry with you," Gateskin explained.

"Yes, we know, Father," Catalina sighed and hung her head, not meeting her father's eyes.

"I agree Father. I know what we did was wrong. We won't do it again until you say we can," Simon added.

"Can we do it again though sometime?" Catalina asked with a gleam in her eyes.

Their parents couldn't contain the laugh that bubbled up after seeing the excited look on their youngest child's face. This brought the children to chuckle along after they saw their parents were no longer angry at them.

Serena looked at Catalina and smiled but gave her a wink that she hoped would remind her sister not to say another word about what she had said to Sunniva.

# CHAPTER TWENTY-FOUR

Arubane was feeling more tired and irritable. All he wanted to do was sleep. He ached all over, but at least the messages had stopped. The Wizards must have worked their magic to stop them. He sighed and looked around the room.

His parents were in the kitchen but he could hear them whispering. They knew something but wouldn't share anything with him. He needed to know what was going on and why they wouldn't let him look at himself in the mirror. In fact, they had taken down all the mirrors in the house. *Why did they do that?*

Arubane called out to his parents, "I need to speak with you. Can you please come in here?"

Hotenfaran and Procelina came into their son's bedroom and sat down on each side of his bed.

Procelina looked at their son and sighed, "What is it sweetheart? Are you feeling hungry? Is there anything I can get for you?"

"No, Mother, but thank you. I just want to know why you won't let me see myself. What is wrong? Am I growing ugly or something? My face feels hairy and different somehow. I feel as if I am growing a beard and have hair on my arms and legs too. What is wrong with me?"

Hotenfaran sighed too and explained, "Something is definitely happening to you.

There is a change going on and we think that the messages are responsible."

"Can you do something to stop these changes? I don't feel like a young boy anymore. I feel like I am getting old and tired and I ache all over. I don't like this at all. Please help me!" Arubane exclaimed as tears filled his eyes.

His mother responded with tears in her eyes too, "Oh, my poor baby. We are working on doing something, I assure you. The Wizards are going to destroy the chest and the Medallion and whatever else is inside it that may be doing you harm. Your uncle will bury it as soon as it is destroyed so that no one can ever find it again and use its powers."

"I would like to help destroy it. Maybe if I am the one to do that it will leave me alone and the spell will be broken and I will return to myself again."

Hotenfaran listened to his son and thought over what he had said. "You may be right, Arubane. That may work. I will contact Gateskin and the

Wizards and discuss this more. I'll let you know what they say. Now just relax and rest. Your mother will get you something to drink to calm you down."

Turning to Procelina he said, "Dear, bring him some of your tea to calm him down. Okay? I will be visiting with Gateskin and returning as soon as I can."

Procelina nodded and left the room to work on a potion that would put their son in a calm state until this could be remedied. She missed her young son and wanted him back.

Hotenfaran flew to Gateskin's home to discuss this new solution. He wasn't at home but he sent a message mentally and Gateskin came out of Solinara's workshop right away. He looked up to see Hotenfaran coming toward him in a hurry.

"Is Arubane doing all right?"

"He is quite upset. We haven't let him see himself and took down all the mirrors but he can feel the changes in his face and body. He complains of feeling tired and achy and quite hairy for a young boy."

"Hmm, I see. We are doing all we can to work that out. At least the messages have stopped, right?"

"Yes, he did say he is no longer receiving any. But I needed to share something with you that Arubane suggested."

"I am listening. I know what a talented and powerful wizard he is. Does he have some solution for us?"

"He did suggest that he could be part of this plan to destroy the chest with the Medallion and whatever else is in there. We still don't know what is in there, do we?"

"No, we don't. We have only witnessed the beams of light that escaped. If the Medallion is in there, the beams of light and maybe something else is protecting it until the wizard can come to claim it. If we allow Arubane to claim it, the beams may release the Medallion and allow him to take it out. That may work."

"Do you want me to bring Arubane to the Wizards' home to do this now?"

"I will come with you. Arubane may not be able to fly and we will have to assist him to get there."

Gateskin and Hotenfaran flew to pick up Arubane and bring him to the Wizards. Hopefully this would work to put the chest away once and for all.

Gateskin sent a mental message to the Wizards to prepare for their visit and what they plan to do.

The Wizards opened the vault and peered inside at the chest. It had quieted down and was showing no signs of movement or beams trying to escape. They closed the vault again and waited for the King and company to arrive. They began to discuss how this would be done and if they thought it was feasible. Before they could get into their discussion, Gateskin and Hotenfaran and Arubane were at their door.

The Wizards welcomed them in and they all sat down to continue their discussion together. The Wizards looked shocked to see how old the poor boy had grown. He now had a beard and graying hair. His eyes were haunted, tired and evidencing defeat.

Arubane tried to smile at the Wizards but they did not meet his eyes. He asked, “Can I see the chest?”

Marno, the Head Wizard, turned to Gateskin for approval. Gateskin nodded and the Wizard walked over to the vault with the other Wizards nearby to be prepared to assist if there was a problem.

When Marno opened the vault, Arubane peered inside and reached in to take the chest out. He held it to his chest. It felt warm but was not sending out any messages. Arubane sat down at the table with the others and took a deep breath.

As he held the chest, he felt relief and sighed, “I think it will accept me now if I try to open it.”

"Okay, Arubane. Open it. We are right here in case it tries to harm you." Gateskin responded.

Arubane placed his hands on the lock and it clicked open without an issue. He lifted the lid and saw something unexpected but amazing.

# CHAPTER TWENTY-FIVE

Procelina paced back and forth waiting to hear what was being done with the chest. She was worried about her son and couldn't stay home. She flew to see Queen Solinara to discuss this with her.

Solinara was waiting for her. Gateskin had sent word for her to watch over Procelina and support her during this difficult time. Solinara expected Procelina would be coming soon. If she hadn't come, Solinara planned to go to Procelina's home to keep her calm. The Queen trusted her husband and the Wizards to settle this once and for all.

Procelina didn't have to knock on Solinara's door because she was there waiting for her with open arms.

"I couldn't stay home, Solinara. I was so worried that I couldn't think straight. What is going to happen to Arubane, my dear son?"

"Don't worry. Gateskin and the Wizards and Hotenfaran have everything under control. Gateskin was quite taken with how Arubane initiated this solution. He felt it would work. After all, it was to Arubane that the chest was sending the messages. It wanted him to come and claim it."

"Yes, but what if it attacks him again and he doesn't....?" Procelina broke down and couldn't go on.

Solinara wrapped her arms around her sister-in-law and held on tight all the time whispering, "It will work, please don't worry."

"I want to believe that," Procelina sniffled and wiped the tears with a handkerchief that materialized out of thin air by Solinara. "Thank you. I guess I needed that. I would have soaked your cloak through with all these tears," Procelina said.

"No problem. I am here for you. Why don't we have some tea? It will calm you and we can talk some more. I feel that all will go well and soon Arubane will be back to being a boy again. He will be a teen soon though, Procelina. He is growing up. But he won't have a beard or a hairy body for a little while yet."

"Yes, I agree. I would like to keep him a boy for a while longer though. He will grow soon enough to be a man and maybe even leave us one day. I don't look forward to that though."

"I don't think he will leave Sovorotskina. He will have his own family one day and live here in his own house which will be close to yours. He will always be close by, Procelina. Now drink your tea. Here are some scones and blueberry cake that I made from the berries in the garden."

"Hmm, okay. I always loved your scones, cakes, and tea. No one can make them like you. Even with all the magic I can conjure, mine never come out like yours," Procelina sighed.

While Procelina was talking, Solinara sent a message to Gateskin to find out how things were progressing. She didn't want Procelina to know how worried she actually was.

***

Back at the Wizards' house they all stood in awe as they looked inside the now opened chest.

Inside was a large golden medallion, the Medallion many have searched for over a hundred years in vain. It was held by a thick golden chain and was giving off a golden glow brilliant enough to blind someone who looked at it too long. They all covered their eyes to adjust for they were now seeing the Medallion in their minds where it had imprinted.

Only Arubane was able to continue to look at it. It didn't seem to affect him the same way. He picked up the Medallion with its chain which felt warm and solid but not too heavy considering the size and thickness. He stroked the golden face and it appeared to wake up and look at him from the red eye in the center which held the largest red stone that he had ever seen, a ruby.

Before anyone knew what was happening, Arubane put the Medallion over his head, set the chain around his neck, and sat back with a smile.

Gateskin and the four Wizards perked up and tried to speak at once in warning about placing the chain around his neck to Arubane but it was too late. They feared that this could harm Arubane.

Arubane spoke up, "I am fine now, Father, Uncle Gateskin and Wizards. No worries, see my face no longer has hair and I am a boy again. It has healed me."

Gateskin nodded in agreement but added, "I don't know what it will do to you to keep it around your neck though, Arubane. I think it is safer to put it back into the chest."

"I don't think it wants to go back in. It is finally free and wants to stay with me. I feel a strong power surging through me like never before. I think it is bonding with me and will keep me safe and maybe give me more powers."

"But we don't know what those powers entail, Arubane," Marno said as the other Wizards nodded.

"I am worried too, son. I don't want anything else to happen to you," Hotenfaran stressed.

"I think it will tell me soon what it wants me to do. It cannot make me do anything I don't want to do. I am powerful already and will control it instead of the other way around," Arubane assured everyone.

"You may think that way, Arubane. But we do not know what it is capable of after all this time. We knew about the legend and that it contained powers beyond our comprehension if owned by a powerful wizard, which you already are," Gateskin stated.

"I believe that it was meant for me to find and bond together my powers with those of the wizard who was my ancestor."

"That may be, Arubane. But we must monitor you at all times. It would be best for you to stay here until the Wizards and I can evaluate you and record any changes in you, such as your personality and body."

"What about my mother? Will you tell her that I am better?"

"Yes, of course. I will contact her now and tell her to visit with you so that she can see for herself that you are well," Gateskin said.

Gateskin sent a message to Solinara and Procelina, "Come to the Wizards' home. Arubane is healed and wants to see you."

Hotenfaran sent his own message to his wife, "Be calm and don't worry about anything. I will explain more when you get here."

When the messages reached Solinara and Procelina, they jumped up and ran out of the house and flew to the Wizards' home a short distance away.

Gateskin greeted them at the door and welcomed them in. When they saw Arubane they both cried out in relief until they spied the Medallion around his neck.

"Why is that around his neck, Hotenfaran? Is that what you wanted to share with me?" Procelina exclaimed in alarm.

"Yes, dear. This is what he wanted to do. It healed him as soon as it went around his neck. We do not know what else it can do or if it can harm him anymore than it already did."

Procelina went over to her son and tried to wrap her arms around him from the back of the chair but something was keeping her from getting too close. She felt a warmth spreading all around her son and a field that was pushing her away.

"What's wrong, Mother?" Arubane asked in surprise as he tried to hug her at the same time. "It won't let me hug you. I'm sorry, but I must take this off right away."

Arubane tried to lift the Medallion off his chest but suddenly it was too heavy and wouldn't budge. He looked in horror at his parents, uncle, and Wizards begging for help. "What is happening?"

"We don't know, Arubane. It appears to be bonded to you and cannot be touched. We will find a way to separate it from you. Don't worry. Okay?" Gateskin tried to assure him.

Procelina looked at her husband and sent him a silent message, "Please do something, Hotenfaran. It may kill our son!"

Hotenfaran nodded and worked some spells and waved his hands over the Medallion. Nothing happened. It only appeared to glow brighter, causing him to look away.

Gateskin said, "Arubane, try to take it off yourself."

"All right. I will try, Uncle Gateskin. But suddenly it is so much heavier than it was before. I don't have the strength to lift it."

Gateskin put his hands on the Medallion and lifted it slightly off of Arubane's chest but it returned on its own and stayed there.

Solinara sent a message to Gateskin, "We may all have to work together to release him of it."

"I agree, Solinara. Let's work together."

He messaged the others silently and they worked together sending spells over the Medallion and waited for it to move.

Time seemed to move slowly as they kept their eyes on the Medallion.

# CHAPTER TWENTY-SIX

The dragonets were snoozing again and their parents were keeping an eye on them as they discussed what had transpired earlier with the King's children.

"We should never have let our offspring take off like that with the children. Something could have happened to them and the King would have sent us back to Dragonaria for good."

"Do you really believe that, Madrigal? I don't think he would have done that. He wants to keep us here. We have been helpful to him and also are a deterrent to the other villages who may threaten him and his village. Didn't he share this with us from the beginning?"

"Yes, he did say all that, Izara, but I don't think he would have ever forgiven us if something had happened. His children are precious to him and his wife as ours are to us. We don't want anything to happen to ours either."

"Okay, I agree we will have to make sure something like this doesn't ever happen again."

"Yes, I will make sure nothing does, Izara. I plan to have a long talk with them after they awaken. You should join me."

"Of course, I will. I have plenty to say to them, dear."

"I wonder where the Queen is with our food? She is usually here by now," Madrigal announced.

"Maybe I should fly over there to see if she might have forgotten or is too busy to come. I could carry the pots over myself."

"No, don't do that yet. Let's wait a little while longer. I'm sure she is busy feeding the other animals in their care. We are not the only ones that she takes care of, Izara."

"Okay, I will wait a little while, but once our young ones are awake, they will be ravenous and uncontrollable."

"I know. We will have to make sure they sleep longer."

"How do we do that?" Izara queried with a frown.

Suddenly Madrigal walked out to the door of the lair and looked around, sniffed the air and raised his wings to test the wind. "Do you feel that?" Madrigal asked with a worried brow.

“What? I didn’t feel anything? What are you talking about, Madrigal.”

“There is something afoot. I can feel it. It is strong and powerful. Keep the dragonets inside until I find out what it is.”

“But what are you going to do, Madrigal?”

“I don’t know but I need to contact the King right away. It could be something heading this way. He should be warned in case he doesn’t know about it yet.”

Izara hovered over her offspring in a protective way and looked around her for any signs of danger.

Madrigal tried to contact the King through his mind as Gateskin had used to reach him. He concentrated and sent a message of urgency about impending danger heading this way.

He waited a few minutes and sighed. “I guess I cannot do that like the King can.” But before he could say anything else he heard a message back.

“What is wrong, Madrigal? Are you and your mate and dragonets in danger?”

“Not yet, but I feel something is coming this way, King. I don’t know what it is but it feels strong and powerful.”

“I will come soon. I have something to take care of first,” Gateskin replied.

“Can you also let Queen Solinara know that the dragonets will need to eat soon? They are sleeping at the moment but not for long.”

“Of course, I will let her know right away. Don’t worry about anything. You and your family are safe. I promise you. I will stop by soon.”

“Thank you, King. I appreciate your kindness.”

Izara looked at her mate. “Did you reach him?”

“Yes, he is coming by soon and the Queen will deliver the food also. Sorry to cause you to worry, dear. It may be nothing. But I don’t think so. It is too strong to be nothing,” Madrigal sighed and went outside to look around. He flew around the lair and near the border of the

UT and the Sea of Shakelle. He searched the skies but nothing appeared to be out of the ordinary.

Gateskin sent a message to Solinara and she responded by leaving the Wizards' house immediately. The others never noticed that she was gone because they were too involved with spreading their powers over the Medallion.

Gateskin spoke up disturbing the spells, "Sorry to interrupt your spell, Wizards, but I must leave here to check the dragons. I think they are feeling the powers of the Medallion all the way over at their lair. That is not a good sign if the powers of this thing can do that."

"I don't see how it is doing anything but staying firmly bonded to our son, Gateskin," Procelina stated with discontent.

"We will figure this out, Procelina. Please don't worry. I will return as soon as I speak to the dragons. I don't want them to worry about anything."

"Well, come back soon, Gateskin. We need your powers to complete this circle or our son will be trapped forever," Procelina cried out in dismay.

Hotenfaran wrapped his wife in his arms as she shed more tears just looking at her son back to normal but still trapped.

Gateskin sent a message to the Wizards to try some of their new spells. "I will return shortly. Keep working at it. We will succeed."

Marno nodded and spread his hands along with the other Wizards over the Medallion and concentrated. It began to lift and then fall back down.

Procelina knelt down next to her son and prayed for a way to free Arubane once and for all.

Arubane looked at his mother and tried to touch her hand. "I'm sorry, Mother. I didn't know it would do this. I thought it wanted me to put it on so it could heal me. I wouldn't have done that if I had known I couldn't get it off again."

Procelina reached out to touch Arubane but the force between them was too strong and wouldn't allow them to touch.

# CHAPTER TWENTY-SEVEN

Gateskin flew home behind his wife and they met at her workshop where she grabbed the bags of food for all the animals. She kept shaking her head for not doing this sooner, preparing the food ahead of time in bulk. She had gotten caught up in the issue with Arubane and was trying to calm Procelina. She had neglected her duties. But now she had worked out a way to create all the food for the animals so that she didn't have to do it every day. She called out to the children to help her take the food to the wolves and animals in the barn.

Serena and her siblings had been relegated to their rooms for the day after what they had done with the dragonets. They came out to help their mother and took some of the food to feed the wolves and the animals in the barn while their mother picked up more of the prepared food for the dragons.

Once the children spotted all the bags of food at the other end of the workshop, they exclaimed, "Where did all these bags come from, Mother?"

"I made them with some elbow grease and a little magic from my potions. This way I won't have to prepare any for a long time."

"Wow! That is great, Mother! How will we know which bags to take for the wolves and animals in the barn?"

"They are all labeled, Serena. See?"

"Ahh, yes, I just noticed that. Good idea, Mother."

"Well, go feed the animals or they will come looking for you," Solinara added with a chuckle.

When Gateskin entered the workshop, he lifted the bags and flew with Solinara to the dragons' lair, he whispered to his wife, "I can't believe you prepared all that food. When did you do all that?"

"Our children just ask me the same thing." She explained, "While you were gone to see Arubane earlier. I didn't want to spend all my time preparing food for the animals every day. This way we have enough to last a long time and all will stay fresh because of my potions."

"Well, that is quite an accomplishment, Solinara. You continually surprise me with your talents!"

Solinara smiled and blushed. "Thank you, Gateskin. I learn from my mistakes."

When the King and Queen arrived at the lair, Madrigal met them outside. He was still looking concerned about what was in the air as he met the King and Queen.

"Everything all right, Madrigal? You do look concerned."

"I guess so, King. I still feel that power coming this way. What is it?"

"I need to explain something to you but let's feed your family first. Okay?" Gateskin was already preparing how to share this problem about Arubane with the dragon.

"Most certainly. I am hungry and so are the rest of my family. My offspring are always hungry. I apologize for that. Their appetites will keep the Queen busy daily."

"No problem, Madrigal. My Queen is prepared to handle this issue without a problem. Right, Solinara?"

Solinara smiled and replied, "This isn't a problem for me, Madrigal. Don't worry yourself. I will always take care of you and your family's needs."

Madrigal bowed to the Queen and sighed in relief.

Izara moved away from the dragonets who were stretching and just waking up. Once they smelled the food, they jumped up and moved over to their bowls which were filled to the brim. They were weaning off their mother's regurgitated meals now. They were quickly getting to move beyond the dragonet stage since they had grown faster due to the special food that the Queen made for them with extra protein and minerals.

"It looks like you came just in time. Look at them eat!" Madrigal said with a proud sigh.

"I guess they were hungry. Why don't you and your mate eat too? We can talk afterward," Gateskin stated.

Gateskin and Solinara waited outside the lair until the dragons were sated. They discussed how large the dragonets had become in a short time. It wouldn't be long before they would not be called dragonets.

Madrigal came out first and settled down next to the King who found a tree stump to sit on while Solinara stayed in the background to listen.

"What is happening, King? Is there anything we can do to help?"

"Not at the moment, Madrigal. Let me explain. I think you know about Arubane and his malady."

"Malady? What kind of malady? You mean the messages he has been hearing?"

"Yes. He was growing older day by day. As you know, he is only a boy, not quite a young man yet."

"Yes, I have seen him. I feel that he has great powers though even as young as he is."

"Yes, he does, Madrigal. The reason he began to age was that the chest with the Medallion that you helped us uncover in Ailylene Mountain was sending him messages."

"What kind of messages? What has that got to do with this malady of growing old?"

Gateskin explained about the messages and brought the dragon up to speed on where the Medallion was now around Arubane's neck and couldn't be removed.

"Oh my, that is a terrible thing to happen to that poor boy. He has been through too much already to have this happen now."

"I agree. We are working with all our powers using spells that have been effective other times but they are not working on this."

"Is there anything that we can do to help?"

"I was going to ask you to aid in the destruction of the Medallion once we remove it from Arubane. The powers it holds are too strong and are not to be trusted. It must be destroyed. It did heal him but now it has taken over his body. I fear it may take over his mind next. Then it may be too late to do anything."

"That can't happen, King. He is too young to die."

"Yes, I agree. It could kill him eventually. We cannot say that out loud in front of his parents. They are devastated as it is."

"Of course, I would never do that, King. I am sorry for even bringing it up."

"That's all right, Madrigal. Now that you know about the powers that you keep feeling, you don't have to worry. You and your family are safe."

“I do feel better. I was also concerned about Arubane, you, your family and the rest of the villagers.”

“That is kind of you to think of all of us. We are all a family. That is how a family thinks, Madrigal. Thank you.”

“I do feel as if we are part of your family now, King. It is my pleasure to do anything to help you in any way I can. Please let me know when you need me.”

Madrigal bowed to the King and went back to the lair to explain things to his mate. She was just finishing up cleaning the bowls and her dragonets who had worn most of the food all over their faces.

Solinara nodded to Gateskin and they flew back to their home to share what they knew with their children who would hear about it soon.

Once the children listened to the problems that Arubane was having, they cried.

"Will he be all right, Mother?" Catalina asked with tears in her eyes that kept brimming over.

"We hope so, Catalina. Maybe we should all pray that we will be able to remove the Medallion safely without harming him further."

Gateskin called out to Spindle and Mitteran to come quickly.

The two guards flew within seconds to the King's door and were brought to the Conference Room for an update on Arubane.

"I can't believe this is happening, King," Spindle exclaimed.

"It is hard to believe that the Medallion could do this. I never suspected it would be capable of attaching itself to a person."

"What can we do to help, King?" Mitteran asked.

"Well, I need both of you to alert the rest of the guards and keep watch over the borders as usual. I don't want anyone coming this way. It is too dangerous. Also, please check on Botular and the Quintaroons, and visit the villagers in case they appear anxious about anything. Assure them that all is well but don't tell them about any of this."

"Right away, King," Spindle and Mitteran said in unison.

After his two Head Guards left, Gateskin held his head in his hands and sighed. He knew that it was time to utilize all his powers to combat this power. He knew how dangerous it could be for everyone around if he did this. He would have to make sure that everyone was a safe distance away before doing so.

Solinara could feel her husband's angst and went to comfort him.

"Is it time to do that, Gateskin?"

"Yes, my love. I think it is coming to that time. You know that I have never had to utilize all my powers but I knew there would come a time when I would have to do so even if it could be dangerous."

"Don't worry about us. I will keep the children safe here. You need to work more with the Wizards. Maybe they have found a way to handle this without you doing anything more."

"We will see soon. I plan on going back there now."

"Do you want to send Procelina back here? She may be too distraught to stay there any longer."

"You may be right. It would be better to have her here with you. You can keep her busy."

"I certainly will do my best to keep her occupied while you work with the Wizards and Hotenfaran to come to a solution."

"Keep the children busy here too. I don't want them wandering around near the dragonets or the Wizards' house now that they know what is going on. Stress to them the danger that this could entail if they do."

"I plan to talk to them about this more and to allay their fears about Arubane. They are frightened of the prospect of losing their dear cousin."

"I feel that way too, Solinara. But I can't share that with anyone but you."

Solinara hugged Gateskin and told him, "I love you. Whatever you plan to do is all right with me. You know you always have my support, dear."

"I know, Solinara. I couldn't do any of this without you. I love you too."

# CHAPTER TWENTY-EIGHT

Spindle and Mitteran patrolled the borders of the UT and flew closer to the borders of Votovia to the east, Merona to the south and Amora farther south. Amora bordered Sovorotskina along Mt Amora and Corian Falls.

Gateskin's home was secluded next to Gateskin River while the Wizards, Hotenfaran's, Henno's and Jennara's, the Quintaroon's, and Botular's homes were further away from him, closer to Corian falls and Lake Serena. He kept the dragons' lair tucked in a corner of the land that didn't border any other village but the Sea of Shakelle. It was situated on the part of the land that is shaped like the hand of Noella Province, as it was called. It was safer that way.

The King still did not want the dragons to venture too far into the UT or closer to Amora which was situated next to Parotovina. He trusted the people of Amora and their rulers, King Noderan and Queen Davora, but he did not trust King Kaposkaran and Queen Beregina of Parotovina. They had spies everywhere. The King Kaposkaran had proven time and time again that he and his wife were dangerous to all and only caused havoc every time they sent spies into the other lands.

Spindle and Mitteran flew close together along the border of the UT and discussed the situation about Arubane.

"I can't believe what is happening to this poor boy," Spindle began.

"It is difficult to imagine something like this would result from this chest. Maybe it wasn't such a good idea to uncover it."

"I agree, Mitteran. But now that it is here, King Gateskin must find a solution to save Arubane. I already told him that we would do anything he needed us to do in order to assist him in dealing with this dreadful object."

"What if the King cannot remove the Medallion? Will Arubane ….?" Mitteran could not say what he was thinking out loud. It was too horrifying to envision.

"I know what you mean, Mitteran. I don't want to say it either. But I believe in the King and his powers. He can do anything he puts his mind to and succeed. Arubane is in the best of hands."

"I concur, Spindle. But I am fearful just the same," Mitteran said but stopped talking and pointed.

"What is that?" Spindle asked, following his fellow guard's outstretched finger.

"It looks like someone is coming this way. But who is that? They have wings!" Mitteran exclaimed in alarm.

"I see them. Wait. I think it is the dragon ladies from Dragonaria. But why are they here and now of all times? I will meet them before they get too far into the village."

"Spindle! How nice to see you!" Jelitza called out as she flew closer to the Sprite.

"Hello, Jelitza. What brings you this way?" Spindle asked in a serious tone.

"Are we going to do this again, Spindle? You are so serious. Aren't we friends by now? Are you trying to keep us from landing inside Sovorotskina?"

"No, Jelitza. We are patrolling the borders and need to keep this area open. I don't think it is a good time for you to visit."

"Hi Spindle. What is the problem?" Aharona and Navaeha asked together.

The three ladies' dragons were getting antsy flying in circles as their mistresses talked with Spindle.

Spindle sent a message to the King to inform him of the visitors and asked what he could share with them.

Gateskin responded immediately, "Let them land and come to my home. I will speak with them and find out why they are here." He sent word to the Wizards that he would return as soon as he could take care of some visitors.

Spindle responded to the ladies, "Come this way. I will escort you to the King's home. He needs to speak with you."

"Oh, this does sound ominous, Spindle!" Jelitza teased him. She had a thing for the Sprite but knew whose heart he held dear. This didn't deter her from trying to win him over each time she visited.

Aharona gave Jelitza a warning look which quieted her down for the time being. She instructed the three dragons to find a safe place to wait and have a nap.

Navaeha whispered to Aharona, "What's going on, sister? This doesn't feel right. They always welcome us with open arms. Something must have happened here. Maybe we should go back home. It may not be safe to stay."

"Let's wait and see, Navaeha. No need to hurry away. I am curious about what is going on. Aren't you?"

"Well, yes, but also a little unnerved. I feel something isn't right in the air. Don't you feel it too?"

"Yes, I do feel it. It is getting stronger the closer we get to the King's home. Besides, I want to visit the dragons. They must be well settled by now and enjoying their new home. I wonder if they will remember us."

"Of course they will remember us, Aharona. Dragons never forget anyone or anything."

"I know that. I was only kidding, Navaeha. Let's see what the King has to say. I look forward to having some of the Queen's tea, cookies and those little tea cakes again. They were so delicious, and just the thought of them makes my mouth water."

Jelitza stayed close to Spindle as they flew to the King's home. She kept her eye on him and winked when he looked her way which made him blush, shake his head and sigh in frustration. He couldn't fly fast enough to get away from her.

The King had returned home from the Wizards' house after he received Spindle's message. He wanted to speak to the ladies and assure them that they needed to return home right away.

The dragons dropped off their mistresses and flew back to Skina Forest to find a nice quiet place to sleep until it was time for them to return to the King's house to pick up the ladies. They settled down under an invisibility cloak.

Queen Solinara greeted the three ladies and welcomed them in. She had already set the table with a couple of different cookies, cakes, and tea.

Aharona sighed in delight when she spotted the cookies, cakes and tea and thanked the Queen. "This is so nice of you, Queen Solinara. We are always thirsty and in need of a treat like this. I only wish we could bake like you do."

"It is my pleasure, Aharona. It isn't a problem for me to whip these up quickly. I hope you enjoy them. Did you have a pleasant trip here?"

"Yes, but it is a long way and we are always tired and hungry when we arrive. We apologize for that."

"Well, enjoy these refreshments. If you need more, I will be happy to bring more right away."

Navaeha stated, "Thank you, Queen, but there is plenty here."

King Gateskin came into the dining area and sat down after welcoming the ladies. "It's nice to see you all again, ladies. What brings you this way?"

"Oh, I hope we have not come at an inconvenient time, King Gateskin," Aharona exclaimed.

"Not at all. But we do have an issue that we are taking care of at the moment. It is not safe for you to stay too long because of it."

"Hmm, I don't understand," Navaeha stated with a frown of displeasure.

Gateskin sighed and responded, "Well, it is a long story but it has to do with the chest and the Medallion that is inside."

"I remember that you were trying to find it and used the dragons to assist you," Aharona recalled.

"Yes, we did uncover it and have kept it in a vault until recently. It has been difficult to contain what is inside it."

"Is there something inside it besides the Medallion?" Jelitza asked, curiously.

"Yes, there are beams of light that protect the Medallion from others."

"Oh, are these beams of light dangerous to people?" Jelitza ventured to ask.

"Yes, they are. But we have contained them inside the chest."

"What about the Medallion? Did you take it out?" Navaeha asked.

"Well, yes. It is outside the box now and that is the problem."

"Is there anything that we can do to help you?" Aharona asked.

"No, the Medallion is a danger only to one person so far. But we cannot take a chance to put any of you in danger."

"How would we be in danger and who is the person who is?" Navaeha queried.

"Well, it is difficult to say. I think it is best for you to leave after you have eaten and return another time. I will let you know when it is safer to come back."

"All right. We will finish our tea, cookies, cakes and leave. Is that what you want?" Jelitza said in a gruff and disappointed tone.

Aharona asked, "How are the dragons doing? Are they acclimated to their new home?"

"Yes, they are doing quite well, Aharona," Gateskin answered.

"Yes, they are lovely additions to our village," Solinara added.

Gateskin nodded and sent a message to his wife to hurry them out of here for he had to return to the Wizards' house.

Solinara nodded and stressed, "We don't want you to feel unwelcome. Please understand that this is a serious matter and could put you all in danger."

"I can't say we understand what this is all about but we will leave. Can we visit the dragons first though?" Aharona asked.

The King and Queen exchanged expressions of apprehension.

"What is wrong? Are the dragons sick or something?" Aharona inquired.

"No, not at all. As we already said, they are doing quite well. But they are sleeping now and don't like to be disturbed," King Gateskin added.

"This is all so strange, King. What is really going on?" Navaeha enquired with a frown of displeasure.

King Gateskin knew that it was time to use his powers to quell this right away. He waved his hands over the ladies and smiled. He said, "It is time for you to return home. You have had a nice visit with Queen Solinara and are full of her tea, cookies and cakes. You will call your dragons to come for you and leave immediately. You will not return until I tell you to come back."

The three ladies nodded and finished their tea and desserts, wiped the crumbs away from their mouths and bowed to the King and Queen and said, "It is time for us to return home."

"Thank you for your hospitality, Queen Solinara and King Gateskin," Aharona stated and pushed her sister and cousin out the door. She signaled the dragons to return to escort them home.

Gateskin and Solinara watched the ladies fly away on the dragons and sighed in relief.

Spindle and Mitteran followed them until the ladies were out of Noella Province and over the Sea of Shakelle.

***

Gateskin sent word to the villagers once the dragon ladies were gone that they needed to stay inside until he told them it was safe. He explained, "We are working on some important issues with the chest and do not want anyone injured in case the beams try to escape again."

Silas answered for the villagers, "Thank you, King. I will alert everyone to heed this warning.

We will wait to hear when it is safe to come outside again. Thank you. Blessings to you and your Wizards that you can solve this problem without harm to any of you."

"Thank you, Silas."

Silas added, "Were the dragon ladies just here from Dragonaria?"

"Yes, they were here for a short visit but have returned home now. No worries."

Silas nodded and sighed.

# CHAPTER TWENTY-NINE

Back at the Wizards' house they struggled to keep Arubane safe from the Medallion's powers. They conjured spells that they had used in the past and worked on new ones to deter the Medallion from harming Arubane any further.

Hotenfaran used all his spells on his son to protect him as he watched his son's eyes glass over. He called out to him in alarm, "Arubane, you must fight this with all your might. You are a powerful wizard and can stop this from taking over your body and your mind. You need to call all your powers forward now!"

Arubane's eyes cleared long enough for him to look at his father. His eyes quickly glassed over again as the Medallion's powers continued to increase.

Beams of light could be seen coming out of the Medallion and climbing up Arubane's chest.

The Wizards called out to the King to return now before it was too late.

King Gateskin was on his way there when he received the Wizards' urgent message. He flew through the door of their house without breaking it and looked closely at Arubane.

Gateskin placed his hands around the boy's neck and held them there to stop the beams from climbing any further. The whole room lit up as the King called all his powers forth to combat this deadly spell cast by the wizard to protect the Medallion.

The air around them grew cold then warm as the beams struggled to maintain their hold on Arubane against the powers of the King.

The air began to circulate around the King and Arubane as the Wizards and Hotenfaran struggled to stay in their seats. They were holding on with all their might to not be pulled up and away by the power of the wind that kept building up from the King's hands.

The beams tried to roll over Gateskin's hands, but he only tightened his grip on Arubane's neck as he kept his eyes on the boy's breathing to ensure he was getting enough air around his grip.

Hotenfaran cried out, "Is he still breathing, Gateskin?"

"Yes, he is. I am watching and regulating my pressure on the beams. I am going to push them away once and for all."

Calling out to the Wizards, Gateskin urges, "Bring the chest closer to my hands now!"

Marno and Wassor struggled to get up from their seats without being blown up to the ceiling as they gripped the chest and pressed it against the King's hands as he continued to squeeze the beams and divert them back into the chest.

"It's working, Gateskin!" Hotenfaran exclaimed as he said a silent prayer.

The beams were getting dimmer as they moved back from Arubane's shoulders and into the chest. The Wizards quickly shut the chest and locked it down.

"They are inside, King," Marno announced in relief.

"Yes, I can feel that they are no longer pushing against my hands. The Medallion is now silent too. It is not moving or as bright as before. It has become dull and lifeless which is a good thing," Gateskin said with a deep sigh. "It no longer is covered by spells."

Arubane's eyes were clear as he looked at his uncle and father who were staring back at him.

"Is it over?" he asked with a quiver in his voice.

"Yes, my son. I think it finally is."

"You are free, Arubane. Try to lift the Medallion now," Gateskin instructed.

Arubane lifted the once heavy Medallion off his chest and over his head. It felt light as a feather now.

"I don't understand. Why is it suddenly so light?"

"It was the beams which were put there by the wizard to keep anyone away from the Medallion. Only a relative like you could put it over your head and use its powers. But unfortunately, its powers were trying to take over your body and mind and rule you."

"Was that what it was intended to do?" Arubane asked, confused.

"It may or not have been. The beams appeared to be getting stronger and having a mind of their own beyond what the wizard intended," Gateskin replied.

"Well, I never want to see that thing again!" Arubane, exclaimed, his face showing his relief as it returned to his healthy glow.

"Thank you, Gateskin, for saving my son!" Hotenfaran cried out as he hugged the King and wept.

Arubane joined his father in hugging the King and said, "Thank you, Uncle. You stopped it from taking over my mind. I would have been lost forever."

"It is what I needed to do. No one could have done that but me. I couldn't let my nephew be taken over by such evil. It certainly was evil that held the Medallion in place."

"You are right, Gateskin. No one could have had the power to do that. We had tried everything in our powers to contain it but nothing worked. Thank goodness you used all your powers to do this," Marno stated as he looked at his fellow Wizards who nodded in agreement.

"I fear sometimes that all my powers may harm those around me. That is why I do not extend them more than I have to. But in this case, I needed to do so and it worked well and didn't harm anyone. Did it?" Gateskin grinned as he looked around at the Wizards and Hotenfaran to ensure they were all right.

"We are all fine, King. No worries. Now what are we going to do with the Medallion and the chest of beams?"

"We cannot put them together, Marno. That is for certain. They are dangerous together. The Medallion is quiet all by itself. We can keep that separate in another chest in the vault. The chest with the beams will be destroyed."

"How are we going to destroy them?" Wassor asked.

"I have a way. Come with me, Wizards. Hotenfaran, you take Arubane to my home where your wife is waiting to hear the news. Stay there until I return."

"You don't have to say that twice, King. We are on our way. Right, Arubane?"

Arubane joined his father in flight to the King's home where his mother would be relieved and happy to see them both.

Gateskin spoke to the Wizards, after father and son departed, to explain what he planned to do with the chest.

"We are going to visit the dragons. I have already spoken to Madrigal. He will be ready to help us destroy the chest. Come. We cannot waste any time getting this done."

Marno and the three Wizards flew behind Gateskin as they held tightly to the chest on the way to the dragons' lair. They whispered back and forth. "I hope this works. What if it doesn't?"

"Stop worrying, Wizards," Gateskin announced in their minds, much to their surprise.

They nodded as the King looked back at them after they landed outside the lair and waited for Madrigal to come out.

Gateskin called out to Madrigal, "It is time to do what I asked of you before."

Madrigal came out and flew around before settling down in front of the King and Wizards.

"Is this the chest with the Medallion?"

"Well, it is the chest but not the Medallion, Madrigal. That is in another safe place. This chest contains beams that are evil and dangerous to anyone who gets near them."

"Are my family in danger being this close to them?"

"Not at all, Madrigal. I would never put you and your family in danger. We need to bury this deep inside the mountain where it was found, but first you must burn it down to ashes if that is possible."

"I will do my best but we will have to move closer to the mountain first. I will dig a hole deep enough to put the ashes in and then bury them."

Gateskin agreed and all flew behind Madrigal to Mt. Ailylene where it all began.

# CHAPTER THIRTY

Back at the King's home, Procelina was hugging her husband and son and couldn't stop crying. "I can't believe it! Gateskin did it!"

"Of course he did, Mother. He is the most powerful and grandest wizard who ever lived!" Arubane gushed over the feats of his uncle.

"Well, I guess you are right, Arubane. I am so relieved. I have been praying nonstop for you to be safe from its clutches. It was so frightening. I thought I was going to die if you…."

"Mother, I am fine. In fact, I feel stronger than ever. It did make me stronger than I was before. That is strange though, isn't it?" Arubane mused.

"Yes, that is odd," Procelina said as she exchanged a questioning look with her husband.

Hotenfaran shrugged and smiled at her to allay her fears. "He is fine, dear. No worries, okay?"

"All right. I am just so relieved to see you back to a boy again. I didn't like the hairy face you had." Procelina giggled as she clasped her son's boyish face in her hands and kissed him on both cheeks.

Solinara smiled as she brushed away a stray tear. She waited until Procelina had enough hugs and kisses with her son and stepped closer to Arubane to give him a huge hug too. She sighed and said, "I am so happy to see you back to your old self or young self, I should say, Arubane. You are as handsome as ever!"

"Thank you, Aunt Solinara. I am happy to be back to myself again. It was quite scary and I felt so helpless to stop it from happening to me. Uncle Gateskin was marvelous to do what he did. No one could have done that! I will be forever indebted to him for saving my life."

The three cousins were waiting in the wings until given the okay by their mother to come forward to hug Arubane.

Serena arrived first and gripped Arubane tightly in a hug as she said, "Thank goodness you are back to normal. I didn't want to see you as an old man before your time."

"No, I didn't like it either. Even though I never got to see myself in a mirror. My parents made sure of that," Arubane chuckled.

Simon came next to shake Arubane's hand but then pulled him into a hug. "I am happy to have you back, cousin."

"Happy to be back, Simon."

Catalina was right behind Simon waiting for a turn to greet Arubane. She smiled at him and pulled him down so she could kiss his cheek and hug him. He was so much taller than she.

"You have a soft cheek, Arubane. I thought you had a hairy face," Catalina stated, puzzled.

"Not anymore. I only had hair on my face when I was hearing messages and was controlled by the Medallion. I am now free, thanks to your father. He is my hero."

"Really? My father saved you?"

"Yes, he did. He is the greatest and most powerful wizard of all."

"I agree. I think he is too! He is my hero also, Arubane!" Catalina said, proudly.

Solinara announced, "Let's celebrate by having a special dinner together. Procelina, let's get cooking to whip up something spectacular for our families. I will also make a few pies from all the berries the children picked recently."

Procelina nodded to the Queen and hugged her son one more time before going to the kitchen to join Solinara in whipping up or conjuring a spectacular dinner to celebrate her son's life being saved.

Procelina sighed heavily and wiped her eyes again with a handkerchief she pulled out of mid-air. She blew her nose and made the handkerchief disappear as she smiled at Solinara who was keeping her eyes on her sister-in-law. Solinara was worried that Procelina was still in shock and wouldn't calm down for a while.

Solinara knew that conjuring and cooking were the best things for Procelina to keep her mind busy and lessen the stress that she had been under worrying about her son.

The two fairies began their conjuring, waving their hands around the kitchen where pots and pans flew back and forth across the grate of the fireplace and wood stove.

Soon the kitchen was sending some enticing aromas of cooking in all directions.

***

Back at Mt. Ailylene, Madrigal worked to breathe fire over the chest from the pit of his stomach. The fire burned brightly but didn't appear to be penetrating the chest walls. He kept trying again and again.

Izara was keeping her offspring busy inside the lair until their father had completed his task. She did not want them anywhere near the chest in case it tried to harm them.

Lorcan whispered to his sister, "Why can't we go outside? I know Father is doing something for the King, so mother said, but we can stay in the field and far away from the mountain."

"I know. But we have to listen to Mother. She knows what can happen to us if we go too close to whatever Father is doing. Just be patient. Let's fly around the top of the lair. I saw some bats up there. They would be a tasty treat, don't you think so?"

"Sunniva, aren't you even a little curious about what Father is doing for the King? Maybe we can help in some way."

"Well, I am a little curious but not as much as you. I would rather stay here and check out those bats on the ceiling."

"Oh boy, Sunniva. You are such a wimp!"

"I am not, Lorcan. You are mean sometimes, brother. Why do you have to be like that?"

"I am not mean. I am just being a dragon. That is how dragons act, curious and …."

"And what, Lorcan? Mean?"

"Hmm, enough talk. Let's go exploring outside. Mother is looking tired. Maybe she will fall asleep. Then we can slip out without her seeing us and go toward the mountain and spy on Father."

"I don't think that is a good idea, Lorcan. What if there is something that could harm us?"

"What is going to harm a dragonet? We are strong and resilient and can bounce back from anything."

"I don't know about that, Lorcan. We haven't had anything to worry about yet. We aren't fully grown yet and don't know our strengths and weaknesses."

"Then maybe it is time that we learn them by experimenting."

"What do you mean by experimenting, Lorcan? I don't like the sound of that."

"Let's find out what I mean, sister. Let's go. Mother is asleep now. We could be back before she wakes if we hurry."

The dragonets flew out of the lair and headed toward the mountain. They stayed out of the way of the King's house and skirted close to Gateskin River and then along the borders of Sovorotskina and the UT. They settled down behind some trees before they reached the mountain to observe what their father was doing.

"See, Father is trying to burn the chest on the ground. It doesn't appear to be working though. Maybe we should help him."

"We don't have fire yet, Lorcan," Sunniva insisted.

"How do you know that? Have you tried to bring up some fire from the pit of your stomach?"

"No, not really, but Mother said we cannot do it yet."

"I think she is just saying that so we won't try it."

"Or maybe she is correct, Lorcan. Why do you doubt her?"

"I don't doubt she means well. She is just trying to protect us, Sister. Don't you know that? That is what parents do."

"Haha, how do you know what parents do, Lorcan? You are only a dragonet, not yet an adult one at that."

"I just know these things. I can feel it here," he pointed to his chest.

"You are too funny, brother. You know nothing about anything. We have a lot to learn. Wait until the King trains us. Then after that you can say you know something."

"Why hasn't he begun our training yet?"

"Well, this thing they are trying to do is keeping him busy, Lorcan. That's why. Besides, Father has been training us every day in his own way."

"I guess so. Well, if we help them do this thing then the King will have time for our training. Right?"

"No, Lorcan. Don't go there!" Sunniva cried out attracting her father's attention.

Madrigal looked up, meeting his offsprings' eyes. "What are you two doing here? Didn't your mother tell you to stay inside until I returned?"

"Yes, but she is sleeping now and we thought you may need our help, Father," Lorcan pleaded as he flew closer to his father.

Sunniva stayed behind her brother and did not meet her father's eyes as she responded, "I'm sorry, Father. We did not mean to disturb you. We can leave now."

Lorcan looked at his sister and shook his head, "No, I don't want to leave until I help Father."

"You cannot help me, Lorcan. You need to return to the lair, now!" he shouted out to them.

"But…I can breathe fire, Father. Look!" Lorcan pulled up his chest and threw it out again with as much force as he could and fire spewed out hitting the chest at the base of the mountain. The chest began to melt before his eyes and dissolve into ashes.

Madrigal added more fires of his own and the ashes burned brighter. He quickly pushed the ashes into the hole he had previously dug inside the mountain and buried it with dirt, small rocks and larger ones to completely cover it. He pushed the final much larger rock over the ashes and pushed it down firmly.

Madrigal stepped back and patted his son on his scaly head and said, "Well, look at that! You can breathe fire. I never could do that at your age!"

Sunniva was awe struck and couldn't speak. She just kept looking at Lorcan and shaking her head.

King Gateskin smiled and nodded back to Madrigal, "Good job dragon and dragonet! That was something to see! You work well together.

Maybe I don't have too much to teach these dragonets after all. They are quite intelligent."

"Thank you, King. But Lorcan and Sunniva disobeyed their mother and will have to be punished just the same for leaving the lair and coming here."

"But Father, I helped you, didn't I?" Lorcan implored.

"Yes, you did, Lorcan, but what if something had happened to you or your sister? I appreciate what you did, but it could have been dangerous for you. Now return home and I will be there shortly."

Sunniva pushed her brother and they flew in the direction of the lair. She kept giving her brother a stern look of warning.

"Don't say a thing, Sunniva. I don't want to hear it!"

# CHAPTER THIRTY-ONE

Madrigal sighed and shook his head. He still couldn't believe his son had been able to breathe fire like that at such a young age.

Gateskin checked over the area where the chest had been buried and said, "Looks good, Madrigal. You did a commendable job covering it up. Thank you. Now we need to keep a watch over it to ensure that it doesn't escape. The beams could still do that."

Madrigal nodded and flew around the mountain and looked down on the area to see if anything was escaping.

"I think it should hold, King. I still can't get over my son being able to breathe fire like that! I am proud but at the same time angry at him for coming here after his mother told him not to. I need to punish him. Not so much Sunniva. She did not do anything and apologized for both of them. She is a sweet dragonet. But Lorcan, I guess he is like me when I was at that age but more talented for sure."

"It is as difficult raising children as it is raising dragonets, Madrigal. I understand your angst. I have felt that way too when my powerful children did something that I was proud of and at the same time made me angry because it could have endangered them."

"What am I supposed to do, King? Do I praise him or punish him?"

"I think you need to talk to him about what he did first of all. Then you tell him that you are proud of what he could do but that it caused you to be fearful for his safety. Tell him that he needs to think before he acts and always listen to his parents who know better."

"Do you think he will learn?"

"Yes, they do learn as we do from our mistakes. That is how we become stronger and more aware of our strengths and weaknesses."

"I see. I understand. I guess my parents did the same for me. I remember being punished a lot. I did learn from all those mistakes. I can only hope that Lorcan will too. Thank you, King, for your wise counsel. I value what you think."

"I am honored to help you, Madrigal. I value your counsel too, my friend."

"We are friends, aren't we, King?" Madrigal hid the tears that he felt brimming at the King's words.

"Yes, I feel we are, Madrigal, the very best of friends."

Gateskin patted Madrigal's colorful wing and bade him goodbye until tomorrow.

The King flew home and Madrigal did the same. They both had tasks to undertake when they met their mates.

The closer Gateskin got to his home he could smell some tantalizing scents in the air. He hurried home for his stomach was growling at him. He hadn't had anything to eat since breakfast.

He flew into the house without anyone noticing he was there. He did a disappearing act so he could go directly to his Conference Room. He had to let his good friend, King Cavelan, know about the chest and its demise.

He quickly opened up the Conference Call to Votovia and saw the smiling face of Cavelan looking back at him. He explained everything that had transpired with Arubane, the chest and how his dragon had burned and buried it in the mountain where it was found.

Cavelan oohed and aahed over every word and then said, "I can't believe you had so much to deal with, Gateskin. I would have been more than happy to assist you in any way I could."

"That is all right, Cavelan. It was too dangerous as it was to involve you too. But it is all done now. We just need to keep a close watch over the mountain range."

"Well, I am relieved to hear that you finally opened the chest and discovered the powers of the Medallion. What are you going to do with the Medallion now?"

"I will keep it under lock and key until I decide what else to do. I don't want to look at it for now. It is too much a reminder of what almost happened to my nephew."

"I understand. Do you plan to inform the other rulers soon?"

"I will eventually. Right now, I am planning on having a celebratory dinner with my family and my nephew and his parents too."

"I can understand that. You have much to celebrate, Gateskin. Well, take care and keep in touch. I am here if you ever need me."

"Thank you, Cavelan. Now I have to get back to my family. My wife is cooking up a storm and it is driving me crazy with hunger. Give my best to your wife and children. Talk to you soon, my friend."

"You too, Gateskin. Take care."

***

Back at the dragons' lair, Madrigal took Lorcan aside after Izara was finished scolding him for leaving while she was sleeping.

Lorcan kept his eyes down as his father explained how he felt. “I did not want you to be injured, son. Do you understand that?”

“Yes, Father. I understand.”

“But I was proud of what you could do. I couldn’t believe that you could breathe fire at this time. You are so young to be able to do that. I couldn’t do that myself at your age. I had to learn slowly.”

“Did I do good, Father?”

“Yes, you did. But you must understand that when we tell you to do something you must obey. We know what is right for you and what is safe.”

“I understand. But I wanted to help you, Father. You were having a difficult time and I knew I could do something to help.”

“Did you know that you could breathe fire already?”

“Not really, but I know if I try hard enough, I can do anything I put my mind to.”

"Is that right, Lorcan? Did you put your mind to doing that?" Madrigal asked with a grin.

"I could probably breathe fire too then if Lorcan can, Father. Right?" Sunniva asked as she raised her scales above her brows in anticipation.

"You probably could, Sunniva. I think you can do whatever you put your mind to also."

Madrigal pulled his son and daughter under his wings and hugged them. He hid the tears that threatened to fall. He loved them so fiercely like he never imagined he would.

Izara looked over at him and grinned. She knew what he was thinking. She nodded and joined the group hug.

Lorcan's stomach growled and he looked around at his empty bowl. "Are we going to be fed tonight, Mother?"

"Of course, you are soon. The Queen is busy with her own family. I will send a message to the King and he will take care of your needs. I guess breathing fire made you hungry, son."

Gateskin received Madrigal's message and told his wife that he would pick up the dragons' food and deliver it right away. He knew she was too busy to do that right now.

He would bring extra food for Madrigal to give to his son for his efforts to burn the chest.

Solinara had told Gateskin that there was plenty of food in her workshop for him to fill all the dragons' bowls for many days ahead due to her efforts to create the abundance needed. She sighed in relief.

Solinara had to think of another way of distributing the food to the dragons and other animals. They all spent too much time doing this. There had to be another way to get the distribution done each day. Solinara would find time somehow in between all the things her husband had to do to speak with him about this. Maybe Gateskin had some suggestions.

The children helped their father pick up the bags of food for the dragons and then went their way to deliver some to the wolves and barn animals while Gateskin flew to the dragons' lair. All the animals were waiting when the children brought the food to the huts and barn.

The royal children hurried to finish distributing the food so they could feast themselves on their mother's smorgasbord of food. There would be much celebrating tonight.

When Serena went inside to eat, she asked her mother, "Can Spindle come and celebrate with us? You know how much he loves your pies."

"Of course. Call out to him and Mitteran. I'm sure they are hungry too and should be celebrating with us."

Serena didn't waste a second to send a message to Spindle which he received and responded in another second. "We are on our way there, Serena. Thank your mother for inviting us. We were starving and could smell the aromas of the food all the way to Skina Forest where we were checking over the borders."

Spindle and Mitteran joined the family and feasted and celebrated. They were even promised to take some leftovers home to their own families afterward.

All was quiet across the village but soon it would not be so.

# CHAPTER THIRTY-TWO

Botular wanted to hear about the comings and goings around the village. He couldn't discover this for himself because he was still home under lock and key.

He hadn't been forgotten and wasn't going hungry because his food kept appearing while he was sleeping. Someone had come and gone without making their presence known. But he knew what he wanted – to find out what he was missing. He was sure it had something to do with the dragonets.

He tried to message the King by thinking out loud about leaving his house. He was sure that the King had him on his mind at all times and would respond.

A short time later he heard a knock at his door. He opened it and looked around but saw no one there. He closed his door and he heard the knock again.

He once again opened the door to let someone know that he wasn't at all pleased with being disturbed. He suddenly realized that he could open his door without help from the King or his Head Guard, Spindle.

He was going to step outside but then felt a wind over his head and looked up to see Spindle grinning down at him.

"About time you looked up, Botular," Spindle announced.

"I didn't see you there, Spindle. What do you want?"

"Didn't you realize that you could open your door without any help?"

"I just realized that. You did help me open it though, didn't you?"

"Yes, I did. Now what is it that you want from the King? He sent me over here to check on you."

"I wanted to go outside. I have been stuck inside too long now. Something is going on and I want to know what it is?"

"Well, if you want to go for a stroll, I will take you. But you will need to return home afterward."

“I figured as much. Thanks a lot,” Botular stated with a snort. “Can you at least tell me what is happening around here? Am I in any danger from the dragons?”

“I can share with you that the dragons are in their lair and you are not in any danger from them.”

“But what is happening around here?”

“What do you mean, Botular?”

“I felt something, and a change in the air. Something that was powerful.”

“Something that was powerful? What do you mean?”

“I don’t know. If I knew I wouldn’t be asking.”

“Hmm, I see. I will have to ask the King what he wants you to know.”

“Doesn’t he trust me yet?”

“I don’t think he ever will, Botular. You haven’t shown yourself to be trustworthy in any way.”

"But I have. I could have sent messages to King Kaposkaran about the dragons and whatever else was going on around here. But I didn't." After he said this, he realized that he didn't have a clue what was going on around the village to share anyway.

Spindle sent a message to the King and waited to learn what he could share with Botular.

Botular stood at his door looking at Spindle who was definitely conversing in his head with the King.

Spindle smiled down on Botular and said, "Step outside, Botular. Let's take a walk around the village so we can talk."

"Will you be sharing something with me finally?"

"You will find out soon enough."

Botular followed Spindle as the Sprite flew over his head and kept looking down at him.

As they passed the other houses next to Lake Serena and Corian Falls, people were out and waving at them. The villagers were out in their fields and called out to Spindle, "Is everything all right?"

Spindle nodded, waved and gave them a thumbs up. They smiled and went back to working in their fields.

The villagers had received a message earlier from the King that the danger with the chest had been averted and that they were safe from any danger of the beams. They were happy to hear this but also intrigued as to how this was accomplished.

They had heard some noise on the other side of Mt. Ailylene but could not see what was causing that. Silas promised them that he would find out more information when he could. He was also interested in learning what caused the chest to send out the beams again. It was supposed to be under lock and key inside a vault in the Wizards' house.

The villagers watched Spindle and Botular travel around their village as the Sprite shared a little about the chest being destroyed and buried with Botular, just enough to convince him that he was safe and there was nothing to worry about. He didn't share anything about the messages or what had happened to Arubane. The less he knew the better. Too much knowledge shared with Botular was dangerous.

Botular pondered what Spindle had told him and then asked, "What about the dragonets? Any new developments with them? I haven't met them yet. Can we possibly pay them a little visit, Spindle?"

"I don't think this is a good time to do that, Botular. There will be another time for a visit."

"But why not now?" Botular pushed for an answer.

"Because the King has given me orders, and I always do as he commands."

"But…"

"No buts, Botular. Now let's get you back home. There will be plenty of time for you to meet the dragonets. The King has to do his training with them first."

"Oh, is that why I cannot see them yet?"

"Yes, one of the reasons."

"What's the other reason, Spindle?"

"Botular, walk this way and don't ask another question," Spindle ordered in a strong voice, forceful enough to quiet a former spy.

Spindle made sure that Botular was locked inside his house before leaving to report back to the King. He kept shaking his head at the nerve of Botular and all his questions. The man never gave up.

After Spindle left, Botular stewed about not being able to learn more but would not give up. He was determined to learn what was really going on around here.

# CHAPTER THIRTY-THREE

Back on Dragonaria, the dragon ladies settled down in Aharona's hut and discussed what had happened on Sovorotskina. They realized that they couldn't remember a thing about their trip there.

They looked at each other and sighed, "What happened over there? Do you remember anything at all, Navaeha and Jelitza?" Aharona asked.

"Only that we had the delicious cookies, cakes and tea and had a nice visit with the Queen, Navaeha."

"I can't believe we flew all the way there and can't figure out what happened during our visit. Did you ask your dragons about this?" Aharona queried.

"No, I hadn't thought of that. Maybe they have some answers for us," Jelitza sighed.

"I did do that before I let Callum take a nap," Aharona noted.

"What did he say?" Navaeha asked, intrigued.

"Well, he doesn't remember anything after his nap in Skina Forest."

"Really? All they did was sleep and then wake up to bring us home? They don't remember anything else?" Navaeha asked, then sighed in exasperation.

"Do you think that the King put us in a trance with one of his spells?" Jelitza inquired.

"Most definitely he erased our memories of our visit there, short as it was," Aharona replied with certainty. "The question is, why did he do that? What didn't he want us to know or see?"

"We should go back again, sister. Shouldn't we?" Navaeha stressed.

"Maybe, but not yet. It is too soon to do that. Besides, I am tired and need to rest first and eat a big meal. I am suddenly starving. Whatever he did to us made me famished more than usual."

"You are always hungry, Aharona," Navaeha chortled.

"I know how you feel. I feel the same. Maybe he did do something to us to cause such hunger," Jelitza added.

"Well, whatever caused it, let's go get something to eat. Mother must have cooked something good today."

"Not Mother, Navaeha! She hasn't cooked since she hired Matilda."

"You are right. Sorry about that. I have really lost my memory. That's not good!"

"Haha, maybe that's just you, Navaeha!" Jelitza joked. "You do have a tendency to forget things."

"Watch out, little cousin. I will remember what you said just now."

"Am I invited to dine?" Jelitza asked, careful not to cause her cousin any further indignation.

***

In Parotovina, the King paced his Conference Room and called out to his guards. "Come here now. I need to plan something important."

When the four castle guards came forward, he asked, “Why are you all here? Who is guarding my castle door?”

“Sorry King. We thought you wanted all of us at once. You did sound anxious and in need of all of us.”

“No, you idiots. Two of you stay here and the other two go back to the front door and keep your eyes and ears out for anything out of the ordinary.”

“What are you looking for, King?” one guard dared to ask.

“Get back to your post and don’t ask me any more stupid questions.”

The guards nodded, shrugged their shoulders and raced back to their post.

The two guards left stood in place and didn’t utter a word for fear of punishment or banishment. They waited a few more minutes before the King spoke.

"I have heard some rumors that there is something going on in Sovorotskina."

The guards exchanged wary glances but didn't respond or ask anything.

"You want to know what is going on, correct?" The King smiled at the men and enjoyed their discomfort. He liked to intimidate his men whenever he could.

The men nodded their heads and then bowed, avoiding the King's eyes.

"Well, I will tell you. There is a rumor that the King had some difficulties with the Medallion. Some beams may have escaped from the chest with the Medallion." The King had heard the Sprites whispering in the trees about a Sprite that was injured by one of the beams.

They nodded and waited for more information. They had no idea what the King wanted from them.

He looked at the men who refused to say a word.

"Aren't you a wee bit curious about this medallion?"

The men shook their heads and lowered them to look at the ground.

"Well, I am curious about the Medallion and want to obtain it for my own treasure chest. I will need you to go there and get it for me."

The men's eyes grew wide in disbelief.

"You are wondering how you are going to do this, right?"

The men nodded.

"You will have to go undercover in peasant's clothes so you will blend in with the other villagers. You will ask around about the Medallion and where it could be. You will find it and bring it back to me."

One guard, braver than the other, ventured to ask, "How will we know where to look for the Medallion, King?"

"You will ask about it and take what clues you can to figure that out."

"What if we can't find it, King? What do we do then?" the daring guard asked.

"You will find it and not leave there until you do. Do you understand?"

The two guards nodded in unison. They waited for further instructions.

"What are you waiting for? Get changed and leave now! I want you back as soon as possible."

The two guards answered, "Yes, King Kaposkaran."

They hurried home to share with their families that they had to leave on another mission for the King. They knew that if they were unsuccessful, their families would be punished or killed. They hurried to dress in their poorest clothes and left the village to travel to Sovorotskina. They planned to take the shortest route there over Crotesia Mountain through Amora, and using a small boat to pass by the borders of

Sovorotskina over the Sea of Shakelle and into the UT.

They would need to skirt around the border of Sovorotskina until they arrived at Mt. Ailylene where they could hide out until it was safe to enter the village.

They were hoping to convince the Sprites in the trees around the village to take pity on them and allow them entrance through the borders that were covered by spells. They would tell the Sprites a story about how they got stranded in the UT and were being hunted by the Catlings.

Once inside the borders, they would blend in and keep their ears and eyes open for any news about the Medallion.

# CHAPTER THIRTY-FOUR

Spindle received word from his fellow Sprites that there were two strangers roaming around in the UT heading toward Mt. Ailylene. They said they would keep an eye on these two to prevent the Catlings from attacking them until Spindle arrived.

Spindle passed the word to King Gateskin that he suspected these two men could be from Parotovina who came to spy on them again.

King Gateskin replied, "Keep an eye on them and get them across the border. I am on my way there. I need to have a little conversation with them."

Gateskin finished what he was doing in his Conference Room and headed over to the village. Many of the villagers were gathered around the men who now stood there wary of what would happen to them. The Sprites had opened up the border and allowed them to enter but not move from there until the King would arrive.

The two men wore expressions of fear as they met the King's eyes. He told them, "Sit down. I think you have something to share with me."

The men looked dumbfounded and didn't know what to say. They just stared at the King and shrugged their shoulders as they sat down on the ground.

"I'm sure you have something to share with me. Are you from Parotovina? Did King Kaposkaran send you here?"

The men nodded finally after the King stared at them, delved into their minds and uncovered their thoughts. "I thought so. What did the King want you to do this time?"

One man sighed and answered, "He said he wanted us to find the Medallion and bring it to him."

"What was he going to do with it?"

"We don't know, King Gateskin. We only need to find it and bring it back or he will kill our families and us too." The man broke down in tears.

"I see. I know what a demanding king he is. Unfortunately, you will never find *the* Medallion no matter how hard you look."

"But we must bring it to him. What are we going to do," the other man begged.

"I will give you something else to take back. It will look like a medallion but won't be *the* Medallion. He will never suspect that it isn't what you say it is. But you must stay here a while and not return too quickly or he might suspect something."

"Where are we to stay and how long? When we do return home, what if our king finds out that this is not the real medallion?"

"I will take care of where you will stay and then let you know when it is time for you to return home. You will not remember any of what I am telling you. You will only remember that you found this medallion at the base of Mt. Ailylene, that is all."

The two men frowned and didn't know what to say in response to the King's confusing words.

"Do you understand what I am saying?"

"I guess so," the men responded.

"Okay, put your hands out in front of you and close your eyes." King Gateskin placed a medallion, that he conjured out of thin air, in the hands of one man. The King waved his hands over the men's head to erase their memories of his previous words. He instead placed the words, "We have found the Medallion, King Kaposkaran, that was buried at Mt. Ailylene."

The next thing the men remembered was that they had retraced their steps and were back in Parotovina entering the King's castle. They had no recollection of how long they had been gone either, which was a few weeks' time. King Gateskin had put them into a trance and kept them that way until he felt it was time for them to return home.

The guards outside the castle escorted the two fellow guards to the King's Conference Room where King Kaposkaran was waiting to hear the news. The King had seen them returning to the village.

"Well, what do you have for me, men?"

One guard stepped forward and held out the fake medallion in his hand. “Here it is, King.”

“Is this *the* Medallion? You managed to find it?”

“Yes, we found *the* Medallion.”

“Did you run into any trouble? Did anyone see you taking it?”

“No, no one saw us, King. We found it at the base of Mt Ailylene.”

“It was just out in the open?”

“Well, we had to dig for it a little,” the other guard explained as he looked perplexed at his own words.

The two guards looked at each other and shrugged their shoulders. They were at a loss for words now and tried to remember what and how they had done this task.

“Why do I feel that you are not telling me everything?”

“I don’t know, King,” one guard stated with a wrinkled brow.

"Why are you looking so confused?"

The guards exchanged wary expressions and shrugged their shoulders again.

"Sorry, King, but we don't remember anything else. We just came back here as soon as we could."

"Hmm, I see. You are dismissed if you can't share anything else with me."

"Thank you, King," they sighed, quickly left the castle, never looked back and returned to their families.

The King kept turning over this fake medallion in his hand. It was plain and didn't have any marks on it which was strange. It had been buried for a long time by a wizard. It should at least be scratched and dirty. Why was it so clean and shiny?

He opened a window to King Gateskin's portal. He planned to ask the King some questions about the Medallion but would not share that he had it in hand. He wanted that to be a surprise which he would enjoy and would relish seeing the shock on Gateskin's face when he told him.

Gateskin heard the sound of a window opening in his Conference Room and hurried there to see who was calling him. When he arrived there, King Kaposkaran's face was smiling at him.

Gateskin chuckled to himself, for he knew why the King was so pleased with himself.

"Well, this is a surprise to see you looking so chipper, Kaposkaran. What did I do to have the honor of your call?"

"Good to see you too, Gateskin. I was wondering about *the* Medallion. Did you ever uncover it, and where is it now?"

"As a matter of fact, I did uncover it but had to rebury the chest to protect my village."

"You reburied it? Why did you do that?" Kaposkaran guffawed as he hid the shiny medallion in his hands.

"It was quite dangerous to my people. That was the only way to protect my village."

"But what if someone uncovered it again?"

"That would not be advisable, Kaposkaran."

"Please explain yourself, Gateskin."

"Hmm, well, we had some difficulties with it. There are beams that shoot out of it and can harm everyone in the way. One beam shrunk a Sprite recently."

"Shrunk a Sprite?" Kaposkaran asked in horror, thinking back over what he had heard from the Sprites.

"Yes, it took a lot of spells to bring him back to normal. It was quite serious." Gateskin tried to keep a straight face.

"But…but, will it harm me if I touched it?"

"I don't think you have to worry about that, Kaposkaran. You won't be able to find it to touch it."

"What if I did find it and touch it?" Kaposkaran's voice raised in alarm.

"Well, who knows. Terrible things could come your way and may even harm your family if you brought it close to them."

"Would it be a good idea to keep it buried then?"

"Oh, definitely, it would be a good idea to do that."

"I have to go. I have important things to do, Gateskin. Goodbye."

Gateskin closed out the window and laughed so hard that he cried. This brought Solinara in to see what was happening.

"Are you all right, dear? You look quite happy but are shedding tears at the same time."

"I know, Solinara. It was too much to hold in any longer." He explained everything that had happened with the Parotovinan guards, the fake medallion he had given them and what King Kaposkaran has shared with him now that he had it in hand.

Solinara chuckled and congratulated her husband on his cleverness in handling a sticky situation.

# CHAPTER THIRTY-FIVE

Back in Parotovina, Kaposkaran raced around the castle and tried to find something to put the fake medallion in and then wipe his hands of it. He called out to the guards to come help him bury it somewhere in the village far away from everyone.

The guards brought in a metal chest and King Kaposkaran dropped the fake medallion into it and closed it with a lock. He instructed them, "Bury this chest far away from our village on the outskirts as quickly as you can. Put a marker there so we will know where it is. I do not want anyone near it. Do you hear me?"

"Yes, King Kaposkaran. But what is wrong with it?" one guard dared to ask.

"Never mind. Just do as I say."

The King returned to his Conference Room and sat to think over what could have happened to him or his family if he had taken it near them. He shivered and sighed.

The guards did as they were told but discussed this and said, "I don't know if our king is going insane. He has spoken often of a medallion and wanted to take possession of it. Is this the one he was speaking of?"

"Maybe it is. It must be tainted in some way. I don't want to know. Maybe it can harm anyone who touches it. Did you touch it?"

"No, I let King Kaposkaran put it into the chest."

"That's good. He looked afraid of it and couldn't put it down fast enough."

Word got around the castle that the guards had to bury a medallion per the King's orders. The other guards were curious about it and discussed this with one another.

"Maybe this medallion is valuable. We could sell it in another village," one guard stated.

"I don't think that is a good idea. King Kaposkaran was frightened by it. It must have some powers that could harm us. He would never bury something so valuable," another added.

"I agree. Let's forget about it. Besides, the King may have our heads if we exhume it."

"I guess you're right." The guards patted down the earth around the chest and walked away. They forgot to put a marker there as the King had instructed.

The two guards who had obtained the fake medallion conversed, "Did you hear that? The King had it buried after we brought it to him."

"I don't understand why he did that? What was wrong with it? I touched it. In fact, I carried it all the way here from Sovorotskina. Will I or my family be harmed in some way?"

"I don't know. Time will tell if any of you are. Sorry to hear that. I'm glad I didn't touch it."

The guard was so distraught that he decided to return to Sovorotskina and find out what powers the fake medallion had over him now that he had touched it.

He didn't share any of this with his family but would leave in the middle of the night and find out from King Gateskin what dangers he had brought to his family.

The guard dressed in clothes that would once again blend well amongst the villagers of Sovorotskina. He followed the same route he had taken with his fellow guard and arrived in the UT by Mt. Ailylene.

The Sprites noticed a man huddled down in the UT and called out to him. "What are you doing there, sir?"

The guard looked up and replied, "I need to see King Gateskin. It is of the utmost importance. It could be a matter of life or death."

The Sprites whispered to each other and sent a message to Spindle to come immediately for they had another visitor.

Spindle was there shortly thereafter and looked down and saw the man trying to hide behind a tree. He kept looking behind him to make sure that there were no Catlings on his tail.

Spindle flew down to see the man and asked, "What brings you here? Didn't you come here before?"

"Yes. I need to speak with the King right away. It is a matter of life or death."

Spindle reached down and lifted the man up with the help of a few other Sprites and dropped him softly into the village of Sovorotskina where he became surrounded by many curious villagers and under the watchful eyes of the Sprites.

"You will wait here. I will speak with the King and return," Spindle replied and flew away to alert the King.

Gateskin was at the dragons' lair preparing to continue with the training of the dragonets once again when he spotted Spindle flying his way.

"What's going on, Spindle?"

Spindle explained about the visitor and what he had said about it being a matter of life or death that he spoke with the King.

"What could this be, King?" Spindle asked, looking perplexed.

"I think I may know what this is about. No worries, Spindle. I will be there in a few minutes. Keep the man occupied and calm."

"Yes, King. I will do my best."

Gateskin explained that he had to leave to take care of an issue. "I will be back shortly, Madrigal. Try instructing your dragonets to fly up and down over currents while keeping inside this area and away from the UT."

"I will, King." Madrigal watched the King fly away and wondered what was going on now. He knew that if the King needed him, he was always ready to help.

The man looked frightened as Gateskin flew near and settled down next to him.

"What is the problem, didn't you come here earlier, sir? You are from Parotovina?"

"Yes, King Gateskin, I did and I am. But no one knows that I am here."

"What is troubling you?"

The man explained that he had given the medallion to his king and that the King had it buried because he said it could do harm to anyone who touched it.

"Hmm, I see. Do you feel any ill effects from touching it?"

"No, King. But I fear that something will happen eventually and may harm my family too. What should I do?"

"There is nothing to worry about, sir. I will caste a spell over you to keep you safe. Once you return home you will touch your family and the spell will be passed onto them to keep them safe too."

"Oh, thank you, good king. I can't tell you how relieved I am. My king would not have been so kind."

"You must not share that I did this or the spell would be broken."

"Of course, King Gateskin. My lips are sealed. I will never mention this to anyone."

Gateskin waved his hands over the man and whispered some unintelligible words as he took the man's hand in his.

The man bowed his head and sighed in relief. "I feel better already, King. Thank you."

"You are welcome, sir. Now I will aid you in returning home safely. Close your eyes and you will be back at home. Don't open them until you don't feel a wind around you."

"Will you fly me home?"

"Yes, in a way. But remember to keep your eyes closed until the wind stops around you and your feet touch the ground."

The man nodded and closed his eyes. He was soon gone from sight. Gateskin guided the man home through the air until he was safely back in the village of Parotovina.

The Sprites cheered as the King smiled back at them. "Keep watch over him, Sprites. He may be a little wobbly after the trip."

The Sprites passed the word to all their fellow Sprites in Parotovina to keep the man in their sight until he was safely inside his home.

# CHAPTER THIRTY-SIX

Madrigal worked with his dragonets to train them to listen to his commands. They were distracted and did not listen well.

When Gateskin returned to take over the training, the dragonets flew back and settled down. They kept their eyes on the King and listened to his every word which surprised their father.

Gateskin winked at Madrigal and smiled. "They sometimes listen better to others than they listen to their parents. My children are like that too," he guffawed.

Madrigal wore a frown as he kept his eyes on his offspring flying around on the orders of the King. He was proud of them but upset that they didn't listen as well for him.

After an hour of instructions, Gateskin spoke to Madrigal, "I want to take the dragonets for a short flight around the village. I think it is time to introduce you and your dragonets to everyone. Call your mate to join us now."

The dragon nodded as he flew back to the lair and poked his head inside looking for Izara. She was flying around at the top of the lair and cleaning out the mess of bats that kept clinging there. Some fell down and were quickly gobbled up by Madrigal while others flew inside the rafters and away from the grasp of Izara. She finally gave up and flew down to see what Madrigal wanted.

"Are you looking for me?"

"Yes, we are going to be introduced to the village officially."

"Really, does the King think our young ones are ready for that?"

"I guess he does. They listened quite well to him, not as well to me though," Madrigal grumbled.

"Oh, really? Is this the first time, Madrigal?" Izara snorted.

"Never mind. We'll discuss this later. Come along, dear, the King is waiting." Madrigal patted her on the tail as she flew by him.

Izara winked back at him and caught up with the King and the dragonets who were showing their excitement about meeting more people.

Gateskin looked at the dragonets and spoke firmly, "Before we go into the village, you must listen to me and do what I say. You will not go near any of the people unless I instruct you to do so. You will not try to breathe smoke or fire to show off your talents. Do you understand me?"

The dragonets nodded and responded together, "Yes, King Gateskin."

Izara smiled at their obedience to the King but not so with her husband who was looking disgruntled once again.

She poked him and whispered, "Get over it, Madrigal."

He snorted and squinted his eyes at his mate in response.

This made Izara stifle a laugh at the expression on his face as they flew to the village.

Gateskin instructed the dragonets to follow close behind him as he hovered over some of the houses along Gateskin River. He waved at the people who came out of their homes when they saw all the dragons flying overhead.

Jennara, Henno, Hotenfaran, Procelina and Arubane came out and looked up at them with expressions of wonder as the four dragons and the King landed nearby.

Gateskin introduced the four dragons to them and told the dragons to tuck in their wings and settle down so the people could come closer to see them.

Hotenfaran was the first to come near enough to look at them and touch the wings of the dragonets after Gateskin instructed the dragonets to lie still and not move.

Procelina came closer too but was not as brave to touch the dragons' wings. Arubane finally moved ahead of his mother and laid his hand on the head of Sunniva who smiled back at him and allowed him to pat her for a few more minutes as he moved his hands along the scales of her neck.

Lorcan wanted the boy to touch his head and scales too and slowly moved closer under the watchful eyes of the King.

Gateskin nodded to Lorcan, "You can let Arubane touch your head too. Be gentle and don't move."

Arubane was so fascinated with the dragonets that he kept his hands on both of them as he walked between them to see their wings and tails that sparkled in the light causing rainbows to dance around them.

Henno and Jennara walked over to the adult dragons and introduced themselves and patted them on their wings. The dragons nodded and were pleased that they were getting some attention too.

Hotenfaran gushed as he thanked the King, "This is such a wonderful introduction to these magnificent creatures. Thank you, Gateskin. They are even more beautiful up close."

The four dragons bowed in thanks and looked at the King for further instructions.

Arubane wanted to stay close to the dragonets. He was smitten as much with them as they were with him. They both licked his hands when he moved away, making him laugh out loud.

The villagers were gathered in the square and waiting to meet and greet the dragons too. They were oohing and aahing as the dragons came closer. The children were jumping up and down and couldn't contain their excitement while their parents tried to keep them away from the dragons until the King said it was safe.

Gateskin instructed the dragons to move slowly forward until they reached the village square where all the people were waiting. He told them, "Be gentle and don't spread your wings out. You may frighten the people, especially the children."

The dragons nodded and crawled forward until they were closer to the anxious villagers.

One child asked, "Can I touch the yellow dragon, King Gateskin?"

Sunniva looked down at the child who walked closer to get a better view of the dragon that glowed like the sun. Sunniva waited for instructions from the King what to do next.

"Sunniva, bend down your head and let the child touch your scales."

The dragonet did as she was told and smiled at the child who was giggling as she put her hand on the scales and moved it over the smooth, shiny surface of the dragonet's head.

The child's mother was close behind her daughter to make sure she was not injured in any way. She held onto her child's left hand as the child kept moving her right hand along the scales of the dragonet's back.

"I think that is enough, sweetheart," the mother exclaimed, anxious to move her child away from the dragonet.

Sunniva licked the child's hand as it came by the dragonet's mouth, making the child laugh in delight. The mother quickly pulled her child away when that happened, not as happy.

King Gateskin responded, "No worries, people. The dragons will not harm you or your children. They are under my command at all times. They will listen to me and their parents and have been instructed to treat all of you as family."

The villagers cheered and clapped at the King's words, looking somewhat relieved.

Silas stepped forward and spoke for the rest of the villagers, "Thank you, King Gateskin, for bringing the dragons here. We have been quite anxious but happy to meet them. We welcome them as part of our village too."

King Gateskin whispered to Lorcan, "You will let me get on your back now and fly back to your lair. I want the people to see how tame you are and that they have nothing to be afraid of. Sunniva, allow Arubane to get onto your back too."

Arubane came forward when he heard the King's words. "Do you want me to fly on the golden dragonet?"

"Yes, Arubane. Would you like to do that?"

"Oh, yes. I was hoping that you would let me do that sometime. I never expected that to be now. Thank you, Uncle."

Sunniva bent down to allow Arubane to get onto her back. Once he was safely settled, she got the word from the King to fly around in a circle over the village to let the people see how safe it was."

Arubane whispered to Sunniva, "Thank you so much. I think we are going to be good friends."

Sunniva nodded and hummed, content.

Procelina watched her son and kept praying that he would be safe and come down without injury. She was still feeling anxious after what had happened to Arubane a short time ago.

Gateskin knew how she was feeling and called to Sunniva to come back down and allow Arubane to go back to his mother.

"It's okay, Mother. I am fine. Please don't worry," Arubane called out to her.

Sunniva nodded and responded to Procelina, "Here he is, safe and sound with me."

Procelina smiled in relief and patted the dragonet on the head as her son alighted.

King Gateskin called out to the people, "It is time for us to return to the lair. Thank you for letting us visit with you. We will visit again another time."

The villagers cheered and waved to the departing dragons as the children called out to them, "Please come back again soon!"

The dragons waved their wings which caught the light and caused rainbows to rain down around the people much to their surprise and delight.

When they arrived back at the lair, King Gateskin said, "Thank you for making this a special time for our village and its people. They were happy to meet you even though they were a little anxious at first. I was proud of you and how well you behaved."

Madrigal spoke for his family, "We were happy to do this, King. We were looking forward to meeting the rest of the village too. I am proud of my offspring. They displayed how far they have come in their training and are growing up to be the kind of dragons that I had hoped they would be."

He hugged his dragonets and licked their heads as they did the same to him. All this display of affection caused Izara to join in and embrace them all.

The dragonets were growing fast and soon would not be called dragonets anymore.

***

Others were feeling left out from all the excitement around the village and would soon let the King know how they felt.

# CHAPTER THIRTY-SEVEN

Serena and her siblings listened to her father describe how jubilant the villagers were meeting the dragons and dragonets. He neglected to mention that he allowed Arubane to ride on the back of Sunniva. He knew that this would not make his children happy.

"Why didn't you tell us about this introduction, Father? We would have been there too to celebrate," Catalina pouted.

"There wasn't time to do that. I decided at the last minute to do that after how well the dragonets responded to my commands. Besides, you had your chores to do."

"All right, but we would have found time to go by finishing our chores faster," Catalina grunted.

Simon poked her in the arm and said, "We can always go visit the villagers and hear what they had to say about meeting them."

"Well, I wouldn't do that just yet. There are a few issues I have to handle before you go there."

"What do you mean, Father?" Serena asked, clearly confused.

Solinara shared his thoughts over the heads of their children and nodded. "I agree, children.

Let your father handle some things first. He will let you know when it is time for you to visit everyone."

"I guess so," Catalina sighed, disgruntled.

Gateskin left the kitchen and went to his Conference Room to call his friend, King Cavelan. He wanted to share how well the dragonets were doing.

The window opened in Votovia in King Cavelan's Conference Room. "How are things going, Gateskin?"

"Surprisingly well, Cavelan. I am pleased with how well the dragonets are doing. I finally introduced them to the villagers who were excited to meet them, though a little anxious."

"I can imagine how they would feel having four dragons heading their way. It must have been quite an impressive sight."

"Yes, I guess it was for them to see the dragons up close. One of the children was brave enough to pat Sunniva even though her mother was not too sure about it. Also, Arubane rode on the back of Sunniva which delighted everyone except Procelina who was still a little anxious of her son's health."

"I can understand Procelina's concern. Arubane must have been thrilled to do that. My wife would have felt the same in both circumstances, Gateskin. I would love to pat them myself as long as you are nearby to protect me."

"That is why I was calling. I want you and your family to visit so you can meet them. Are you ready for that?"

"Of course, Gateskin. I have been waiting to hear when it was safe. My children will be thrilled to come and meet the dragons. My wife will be anxious but I will assure her that it will be safe with you there to protect us."

"Yes, it will be safe. I promise you that. Let me know when you can come so I can let Solinara prepare everything for your visit and stay."

"Please tell her not to go to too much trouble. We don't need much. We will bring some food and everything else we will need."

"That won't make a difference with Solinara. She will go to whatever extremes she can to make it special for you." Gateskin laughed.

"I'm sure, Gateskin. I will let you know when we will be coming. I'm sure my children will want to come right away," Cavelan responded with a chuckle.

Gateskin nodded and said, "We look forward to seeing you and your family soon."

Both kings closed their windows with nods and broad smiles.

Gateskin informed his wife of the visitors who would be coming soon. As he expected, Solinara raced around preparing the large room with fresh sheets on the beds, and with the help of their children, dusted the furniture and swept and washed the floor. She could have done all this with a few waves of her hands and a couple of tidy spells but she enjoyed working with her hands and felt it was good for her children to know how to do such things as manual labor.

Gateskin had created this extension to his home for visitors. He had housed Cavelan and his family there once before when they had come to aid him in rescuing the Taken Ones. He had included many beds, closets, a dining and sitting area and a bathing room too.

While his family were busy preparing for King Cavelan and his family's visit, he called Spindle and Mitteran to meet him at Botular's house.

He flew there and went to Botular's door where Spindle and Mitteran were already waiting.

"Is there a problem with Botular, King?" Spindle asked.

"We will find out soon enough. Let's go in. Don't even knock. He won't be able to open the door anyway."

Spindle unlocked the door and the three entered to find Botular sitting at his table looking guilty.

"Oh, I didn't know you were coming to visit me today, King."

"This is not a friendly visit, Botular. We are here to find out why you are looking discontented. I can feel your ire."

"Well, I am unhappy and feeling neglected."

"Why is that, Botular?"

"I know that something big has taken place in the village. I could hear some cheering going on."

"I see. What do you think you missed?"

"I don't really know but I am curious about it."

"Are you?"

"Yes, King. I am. Why am I not included with anything that is going on around here in the village? I am a citizen, Am I not?"

"Yes, you are a citizen but not a trusted one at times."

"Oh, well, that has changed. I told you I can be trusted. I have promised every time we met that I could be a trusted citizen of Sovorotskina."

"Can you?"

"Yes, King. I can be trusted. Please give me another chance."

"All right. Come with me, Botular."

"Where are you taking me, King?"

"No questions, just come."

"Okay."

Spindle and Mitteran followed behind Botular and the King. They were not sure what the King was planning but soon realized as they saw the lair coming into view.

Botular's eyes grew wide as he saw the massive size of the lair. It towered over all at least forty to fifty feet high and more than twice as wide. He hesitated to move closer even though he was excited and was holding his breath.

Gateskin flew closer to the lair and called out to the dragons to announce their presence.

Madrigal peeked out to see the visitors and flew out to land at the King's feet. He bowed in front of him and hummed in delight to see the King.

The King asked, "Please have your family come out. There is someone I want you to meet. He has been waiting for a long time to meet you."

Madrigal nodded and went back inside, coming out a minute later with his mate and dragonets.

The four dragons looked at the visitors nodding at Spindle and Mitteran who they already knew well. Their eyes stopped at the man who was standing there shaking in his shoes as his eyes met theirs.

"This is Botular. He was formerly from Parotovina and was the eyes and ears of King Kaposkaran."

"He was? Why is he here now, King?" Madrigal asked, feeling perplexed.

"He has promised to be a trustful citizen of Sovorotskina."

"He does? Do you trust him, King?" Madrigal asked as he winked at the King.

"Do you think I should, Madrigal?"

Botular shivered and bowed his head to avoid looking at the fiery eyes of the dragon.

"What do you say about that, Botular? Can you be trusted?"

"I…I…yes, I…can be, King. I promised to be trustworthy from now on."

Madrigal snorted and looked closer at Botular who appeared as if he would faint any minute.

"I think I believe him, do you, Madrigal?" the King said as he winked at the dragon and shared his thoughts to Madrigal's mind about frightening the man.

"Hmm, I think I do too, King. Would he like to meet my family?"

Botular spoke up, “Yes, I would love to meet your family, Madrigal.”

Izara stepped closer and nodded at Botular. The two dragonets came around their mother and stared at Botular.

King Gateskin introduced Botular to the dragonets explaining that Botular came from another village a while ago and is now a citizen of Sovorotskina as the dragnets were.

Lorcan said, “We are pleased to meet you, Botular, since you are a citizen of Sovorotskina just as we are.”

Sunniva bowed to him and said, “I am happy to meet you too, Botular. That is a funny name. What does it mean?”

Botular shook his head, “I don’t know.”

“Well, my name is Sunniva and it means sun gift.”

Lorcan spoke up, “My name is Lorcan and it means fierce.”

"Oh, I see. You do look like a sun gift, Sunniva, and Lorcan looks quite fierce."

Botular's words delighted the dragonets as they smiled showing all their teeth which made Botular take a few steps back.

At Botular's startled reaction, the dragonets began to laugh so hard that they fell over. This frightened Botular even more but he soon joined in laughing when he saw the King's smile.

"Well, what do you think, Botular? Are you happy to meet the dragons and dragonets?"

"Oh, yes. I am most pleased to make their acquaintance."

"Hmm, acquaintance?" Gateskin chuckled over Botular's formal words.

"What's so funny, King Gateskin?" Botular looked confused.

"Nothing, Botular. I think it is time for you to return home. Your dinner will be coming soon. We don't want it to get cold, do we?"

The dragons hearing the mention of food began to drool. Izara escorted them back inside in case they decided they were hungry enough to eat their visitor.

Botular noticed the dragonets' reaction and said, "Yes, I think it is time for me to leave, King. In fact, let's go right now!" He looked behind him to make sure the dragonets were not following him.

Madrigal nodded and bowed to the King and followed his family inside the lair.

Spindle and Mitteran escorted Botular to his house. When they looked inside, Botular's dinner was already there. Botular sniffed the aroma of his food and sat down to enjoy it.

Spindle smiled at Botular who was oblivious to the fact that he was still there observing him. He and Mitteran didn't wait to be dismissed by the King and flew out of the house to return to their homes to have their own dinners. The delicious smells of the food had made them hungry too.

Gateskin watched as Spindle and Mitteran flew to their homes as he headed back toward another house to take care of a pressing matter.

# CHAPTER THIRTY-EIGHT

The two Quintaroons paced back and forth and grumbled to themselves. They knew that the King would be coming soon. They had summoned King Gateskin and were getting tired of being ignored.

They had wanted to change into their creature selves but didn't dare displease the King. They wanted to ask him a favor and wouldn't be able to do that in their creature forms.

King Gateskin appeared at the door of the Quintaroons and came inside without waiting to be asked. He flew right through the door as he could easily do when needed.

The Quintaroons jumped back in alarm when they saw the King appear that way. They had no idea he could do that. This fact unsettled them and they were at a loss for words.

The King stood there and waited, "What is so urgent that you needed to see me right away?"

"We wanted to know what was going on in the village. We could hear cheers and celebrating. We felt left out, King," Quintal stated with a huff.

"Hmm, I see. You and another individual."

"What?" Quintal asked.

"Never mind. What do you want from me?"

"We want to know what was going on in the village. What were they celebrating? How come we are not included in things happening in the village. We are citizens too, King," Taron exclaimed.

"Yes, you are citizens. I don't know if I can trust you to not change into your creatures again. You would harm other citizens if you did."

"We won't do that, King. We have promised not to do that unless you need us to be creatures to aid you in some way," Quintal explained.

"Well, since the other individual has met the dragonets, I guess it is time for you two to meet them."

"Meet the dragonets? Is that what was going on?" Taron quizzed.

"Yes, as a matter of fact, that is exactly what they were celebrating. Are you ready to meet them?"

"Oh, yes!" Quintal shouted louder than he intended as he exchanged grins with Taron.

"All right then, come with me. But you must be on your best behavior for the dragonets are getting hungry. It is almost time for their dinner as well as yours."

"Hmm, we understand, King. But will you stay close by in case they think we are their dinner?" Taron asked as he looked alarmed.

"Of course. I will be the one to introduce you. Come along now. Let's make this quick."

The Quintaroons nodded and walked behind the King exchanging wary looks and shrugs with each other.

"Have you changed your minds?" King Gateskin questioned when he saw the cautious expressions on their faces.

"No, we want to meet them, King. We are just a little anxious, that is all." Quintal answered.

Gateskin called out to the dragons once again. Madrigal responded and was surprised to see the Quintaroons standing there looking panicky.

"I guess this is the day to meet and greet, huh?"

"Yes, Madrigal. I guess it is. Sorry to bother you again so soon, but these two wanted to meet the dragonets. They were feeling left out after everyone else has already met them."

"What? We are the last to meet them?" Taron asked, surprised.

"Yes, you are," King said with a fierce stare, causing Taron to bow his head.

Madrigal brought out his mate and dragonets again much to their dismay. They were not up to another introduction since they were getting hungry and feeling irritable.

Lorcan had a fiery look in his eyes and Sunniva was feeling tired and not up to being as nice as usual.

"Sorry to bother you but the Quintaroons wanted to meet you both. They had heard all the cheering from the village when you were there."

"Okay. Hello," Sunniva said as she looked at the two and turned to go back to her lair and wait for her dinner.

Lorcan sighed and said, "Yeah, hi. See you around." He returned to the lair with his sister.

"Sorry about that, King Gateskin. They are hungry and weary and not up to visitors. They will be better after they eat but then they will take a nap. In fact, I will be doing the same thing. Maybe they should come back another time when we are not out of sorts."

"No problem, Madrigal. I think you and your family have had enough visitors for today," Gateskin responded and pushed the Quintaroons in the direction of their house.

The Quintaroons moved faster and kept looking behind them to ensure they were not being followed.

# CHAPTER THIRTY-NINE

The following day King Cavelan and his family were now on their way to Sovorotskina with all their goods and presents for Queen Solinara and the children. They had also brought some tasty treats for when they would meet the dragons and dragonets.

The children couldn't contain their excitement over meeting the four dragons. They couldn't believe this was happening. They had much to discuss with the children of King Gateskin and Queen Solinara.

When they arrived, King Gateskin opened the doors to the large extension to house his visitors. The children and other family members hurried inside to claim their beds and storage spaces.

Serena and her siblings rushed inside the extension to meet their friends and share everything they could about the dragons and the new dragonets. They went into the play room that the children had where they could discuss all this in private.

Adolphin and his sister, Anatonia Noella, presented the three royal children with gifts that they had brought. There were oohs and aahs as the three royal children expressed their gratitude and how much they loved what they had received.

Adolphin was the oldest child and his sister, Anatonia Noella, was a couple of years behind him. They hadn't been to visit for a couple of years and had a lot to share.

Catalina couldn't contain her excitement at seeing them. She felt grown up now and wanted to show how much she had learned about the dragonets. She did not share what she and Simon had done about watching the eggs hatch. Her sister had warned her about that.

Adolphin was the same age as Serena while Anatonia Noella was Simon's age. They were all teenagers except Catalina who was feeling left out of their conversations.

She spoke up suddenly to get the attention of the others. "I saw the eggs hatch!"

Serena turned to look at her sister and gave her a stern frown filled with warning.

"What? You actually saw the eggs hatch?" Adolphin exclaimed, eyes wide in disbelief.

"Is that right?" Anatonia Noella questioned, eager to hear more.

"Well, are you going to tell us about it?" Adolphin stressed.

Serena interrupted this vein of conversation to say, "We should get something to eat. You must be starving after your journey."

Catalina frowned in disappointment as she left the room to hide in her bedroom. She felt embarrassed and ashamed at the same time. She couldn't understand why her sister wouldn't let her share this wonderful experience she had had.

After Serena got their guests situated in the dining area in the extension with some snacks, she went to see her sister. She knew that Catalina was quite upset and had to try to calm her down.

Catalina was laying on her bed with her head buried under her pillow. Tears leaked out of her eyes and she hurriedly wiped them away when she heard her sister's voice as she entered the room.

"Catalina, let me explain why I did that. I know you are upset with me." Serena waited for her sister to turn over and acknowledge that she was trying to make amends.

Catalina just sniffled and pounded her pillow but didn't turn around.

"Please listen to me. Father did not want you to share this with our visitors. He did not want them to know that he allowed his children to do that. It doesn't make him look like a good father."

At these words, Catalina turned over and looked at her sister. "What do you mean, he isn't a good father? Of course, he is the best father ever."

"I know that and you know that but they won't think that way if they knew what you did."

"I don't believe you. I don't think he would be angry with me if I shared this. I could tell them that I did not get permission from him and convinced Simon to come with me. That is exactly what I did."

"I know. You told me that. But still, we shouldn't share this with them. Let's just say that you wanted to do that and imagined that you did."

"No, I won't do that. It will make me look like a liar or worse a baby." Catalina turned over and lay her head under her pillow again.

"Come out now and we will think of something to say. Please don't act this way. Acting this way will make you look like you are immature and not almost a teen."

"Oh, do you really think so, Serena? I don't want them to think that I am immature."

"Okay, then let's go out and have some snacks. Wipe your eyes and blow your nose. Fix your hair too. It is all over the place from being under your pillow."

"All right, I will do all that, sister. No more bossing me please!" Catalina sighed but did as she was told and followed her sister into the dining area in the extension.

The children all looked up when they saw Serena and Catalina. "Are you all right, Catalina?" Anatonia Noella asked in a soft voice.

"I am fine. I had to…um…fix my hair. My sister said it was a mess." Catalina tried to smile to cover up her sad face.

"Are you going to share more about the dragons?" Adolphin probed.

Serena answered for her sister, "No, she should have explained that she dreamed of seeing them hatching."

"Oh, too bad. I wanted to hear what that felt like to see them come out of their shell. That would have been really something to see."

Simon looked at Serena and shrugged his shoulders and then sighed joining Catalina at the same time.

Simon spoke to Catalina in her mind. He didn't want the others to know what he was saying. He knew that Serena would probably eavesdrop on them.

"I wanted to share this too, Catalina. I'm sorry Serena said that. Maybe we should ask Father if he feels the way that Serena said he would."

"I don't think so. I don't want to remind him about what we did against his wishes. He may decide to punish us after all, Simon. Ssh, just forget about it. Okay?"

"If you say so, little sister. Mums the word."

Catalina nodded and looked over the snacks, picking her favorites and stuffing her mouth so she couldn't answer any more questions if asked.

Gateskin waited for everyone to finish their refreshments and announced, "I will visit the dragons and see if they are up to some more visitors. I brought them to the village and had others who wanted to meet them yesterday. They were all tired out and hungry at that point. I will make sure that they have a good meal and a snack or two before I take you there."

Cavelan listened to the King's explanation and asked, "Will we look tasty enough to make them want to eat us?" He giggled but then stopped when he saw the shock on his children's faces.

"Oh, not at all, Cavelan. They are well trained and never a problem. You and your children are safe with them as long as I am there."

The children exchanged wary glances with each other and then Adolphin asked, "Do you think that we could wait until they are no longer hungry, Father?"

"No, I think King Gateskin will know when to take us there. Don't worry, son."

Adolphin nodded but didn't look too sure about this. He looked at his sister who was staring at him with wide eyes and shaking her head.

Serena added, “They are lovely dragons and so incredibly beautiful that just looking at them will take your breath away. You will be amazed at what they can do too.”

“Really?” Anatonia Noella responded.

“Yes, they are kind dragons,” Catalina added. “We even went for a ride on their backs which didn’t make our parents too happy. But it was so much fun when we flew around. The wind blew at our backs and around us. It was wonderful! I can’t wait to do it again!”

“Wow, I don’t know if I would be as brave as you, Catalina,” Anatonia exclaimed.

This made Catalina feel better and she held her head high and smiled broadly at her sister.

Serena nodded and smiled back at her, happy to see her sister was back to her pleasant self again.

Gateskin excused himself and flew to see the dragons.

What he saw there was something he never expected to see.

# CHAPTER FORTY

The dragons could feel a force that was dark and strong outside their lair. Madrigal looked out and saw a black cloud. It was hovering over the lair.

He went back inside and shared this with his mate. “There is something out there. I fear it is Dark Magic and could harm you and our offspring. You need to cover them with an invisibility cloak and stay quiet. Put them to sleep whatever way you can. I need to check this out further.”

“Get the King here.”

“Yes, I am calling him in my head now. He answered and said he was heading over to see us anyway.”

“Good. Why don’t you wait for him before you do something stupid.”

“What do you mean? I won’t do anything stupid,” he grumbled.

Before Madrigal could get into trouble, he heard the King’s voice talking to someone.

He looked out once again and saw the black cloud change into a woman in a flowing black cloak with silver threads running through it. She had glossy black hair and a face that would be beautiful if it wasn't controlled by evil and looked dark and menacing. He moved out quietly and waited for the King to ask for his assistance.

Gateskin looked at the woman and asked, "What are you doing here, Elowen?"

"Oh, I just thought I would drop in to visit the dragons. I hadn't seen them for a long time."

"You are never welcome here, Elowen. Do you remember the last time you visited? You nearly killed my children."

"You are so wrong about that, King. I would never have killed them, changed them into something else maybe though," she explained.

"What do you want, Elowen? I won't ask you again."

"I just want to see the magnificent dragons you have."

"Well, I don't think they want to see you."

Madrigal stepped forward and called out, "I would like to see this lady or whatever she claims to be."

"Ooh, you are quite handsome. What is your name?"

"I am Madrigal. What is yours?"

"I am Elowen, sister of the two dragon ladies who visit here. I'm sure you know who I mean. They are the ones who brought you here."

"Yes, I know them. They are lovely ladies in the true sense of the word. You on the other hand…I don't know if I would call you…"

"What would you call me, dragon?"

"Anything but a lady."

"Ooh, that is not a good thing to say to a wizard who practices Dark Magic. I could make you into anything that I want."

"I don't think you will though, Elowen. I think you are smarter than that," Madrigal added.

"It is time for you to leave, Elowen. You are not welcome here," Gateskin stressed once again.

A scuffle could be heard coming from the lair and a shout. Madrigal went back inside to see what was happening. His mate was trying to keep the dragonets quiet and was not being too successful.

"Do you need help?"

"No, dear. Sorry about the noise. Lorcan bit me when I tried to hold him down."

"He bit you! I will take care of him." Madrigal grabbed Lorcan by the ears and whispered, "You need to apologize to your mother."

Lorcan looked up at his father who was ready to blow smoke at him and possibly fire. He said, "Sorry, Mother. I didn't mean to do that. I was sleeping when you touched me. You made me jump."

Izara nodded and patted Lorcan. "It's okay. Just go back to sleep. We need you to rest and be quiet for now."

"What is going on outside? I feel something strong and smelly too."

"You smell something?" Madrigal asked.

"Yes, don't you smell it too, Father. It is quite strong and is making me want to gag and upchuck what little I have in my stomach."

"Hmm, that is strange. I don't smell it."

"Really? I thought you were more perceptive than I to outside changes, Father."

"I guess I must be getting old."

Sunniva sat up and opened her eyes. "What is going on? I was trying to take a nap. You are making too much noise, brother."

"It's about time you woke up, sister!"

Sunniva looked around and sniffed the air. "What is that awful smell?"

"You smell it too, Sunniva?" Madrigal quizzed in surprise.

"Yes, it's making me gag!"

Izara added, "Yes, Madrigal, I smell it too. It is quite nauseating."

Madrigal flew outside and sniffed the air as he flew around the lair. He ventured further and kept his nose up to catch the drifts and then he smelled it too.

He flew back to his family and announced, "Yes, I smell it now. It is coming from this woman."

"What woman, Father? Is someone here?" Lorcan asked as he tried to look outside.

"No, do not go near the door. It is dangerous. Stay here with your mother."

The look in Madrigal's eyes sealed his words. His dragonets laid back and closed their eyes after seeing the anger in their father's.

Izara nodded to him and lay next to them with her wings covering them protectively under an invisibility cloak that dragons were capable of doing.

Elowen was trying to pick up what was going on inside the lair. She settled down next to the King and asked, “What is happening inside there? Are the dragons not getting along?”

Gateskin sent a Cover Spell over her to prevent Elowen from moving any closer to the lair. She noticed this and tried in vain to undo this cover. She became belligerent and strained to cast a spell of her own without much success.

“It is time for you to return home now, Elowen, unless you want me to use more of my powers to harm you.”

“How can you harm a powerful wizard who uses Dark Magic?”

“You have no idea the powers that I possess. I haven’t used them all yet unless I need to.”

“That is difficult to believe, King. I don’t believe you can harm me or even want to because my family would be harmed along with me.”

“That may be what is keeping me from doing more, Elowen. I respect your parents and siblings but not you. I think they would understand if I had to do something more to keep you from harming my family and village."

"Hmm, I am feeling unwelcome."

"Yes, you are. This is my last warning, Elowen. You must leave here now and not return unless you want to see these powers and feel their anguish."

Elowen appeared to be musing over the King's words and finally responded, "I will leave but I do not promise that I will not return. My business with you is unfinished."

Gateskin removed the Cover Spell and allowed Elowen to fly away. He watched her leave and sent word to Spindle and Mitteran to keep eyes on her until she was over the Sea of Shakelle.

Spindle and Mitteran were close by and watching the goings on at the lair the whole time in case they were needed. They responded positively, "We have her in our sights and will keep watch until she is out of sight."

Gateskin called out to Madrigal, "Are you all right in there?"

Madrigal came out after checking on his family and said, "Yes, all is well here, King. Thank you for sending her away. I was ready to send smoke or even fire her way if you needed me to do that."

"I know you were ready to assist, Madrigal. For that reason, I am pleased to have you close by. I didn't plan on harming her unless she pushed me to do so."

Izara looked out and asked, "Is it safe for our dragonets to come out now? They need to relieve themselves. I think all this excitement has affected them that way."

Madrigal chuckled and said, "Let them out. All is safe now."

# CHAPTER FORTY-ONE

Gateskin returned home to share what took place at the dragons' lair with his wife. She had sent messages to him because she had felt his anxiety. She was always on the same wave length with him no matter what.

She met him at the door and pulled him into a hug and a deep kiss. He could feel her shaking as she did this and he kept her close until she calmed down.

"Are you all right? Are the dragons safe now?"

"Yes, everyone is safe now that Elowen is gone. Spindle and Mitteran are watching the skies to make sure she does not return. I spoke to both of the guards and told them to find some Sprites who are strong, talented and trustworthy enough to give Spindle and Mitteran some time off. They have been working non-stop."

"I think that is an excellent idea, Gateskin, to give your trusty Head Guards some time off."

"They both agreed to do that too. Spindle has already chosen some of his fellow Sprites who are willing to keep watch over the borders for him and Mitteran when they are off duty. The Sprites always have been our border watchers anyway. Now we will make them official."

"I'm sure they will do their usual best to please you, Gateskin. I'm also relieved to hear that

Elowen left. I could feel your anxiety. It was crushing me not to go to you. I know I couldn't do that. I also believed that you would keep us all safe against her Dark Magic."

"I could feel you keeping me calm. That is what made me stronger."

"Good to know. I will keep sending you my strength that way. We are a team, Gateskin. I am always here for you."

"I know, Solinara. That I know. Are the children inside?"

"Yes, I told them to wait inside until I knew everything was safe."

"I'm sure they have questions."

"Of course they do, dear. Why don't you go share some of what you need in order to squelch their curiosity and keep them content."

"That should do it for now. But I'm sure they will want to know everything in detail," Gateskin guffawed.

Solinara winked at him and went back to taking care of their visitors. She was going to explain to them that Gateskin would be in soon to see them about visiting the dragons.

The visitors were kept busy in the extension by Solinara the whole time that Elowen had been at the lair. She did not want to alarm any of them as to the danger that Elowen had brought with her.

After Gateskin visited with his children and they had stopped asking questions, he went to see King Cavelan to explain the same episode.

Cavelan looked up when he saw Gateskin enter the extension. He could see some strain on his face which was always so stoic.

Gateskin nodded and told him, "Follow me, Cavelan."

Cavelan followed without question and after sitting at the table in Gateskin's Conference Room, he waited for an explanation.

"I must explain what this is all about. I know you can see the strain in my face. It has been an unexpected visitor that has caused me to feel this way."

Cavelan nodded and said, "Please continue."

"Do you remember the woman I mentioned in the past that caused me problems, named Elowen, from Dragonaria?"

"Yes, I do."

"Well, she paid a visit to my dragons. She did not get inside because I put a spell on her. If I hadn't arrived there when I did, she would have gotten her hands on the dragonets and who knows what she would have done."

"Wouldn't the parents have killed her to save their offspring?"

"Yes, I fear that would have happened unless she could have used Dark Magic to stop them."

"Do you think she is capable of deterring dragons?"

"I know the power she possesses when she uses Dark Magic is quite surprising, but the dragons, I'm sure, would have fought back."

"I see. But your powers can handle Dark Magic."

"I like to think so, Cavelan. But she appeared to be more powerful than ever. I think Dark Magic has taken over her whole persona. She is not the same person I saw before. She is darker now and covered in a black cloud. She did come out of it to speak with me but then the cloud covered her again."

"That is not good at all. I see what you mean. Is there something that I can do to help?"

"Not now. She has gone back to Dragonaria. Spindle and Mitteran are keeping watch to ensure that she will not return."

"You are fortunate to have such wonderful Head Guards. Also, you have all the Sprites to keep watch."

"Yes, that is something I never take for granted. They are my little watchdogs. I wouldn't know what to do without their assistance."

"I think we need to let the dragons rest for today. I will bring them food to keep them happy. Tomorrow, we will visit them. I didn't even mention when I was there that I had some more visitors for them to meet."

"That is not a problem. Everyone is settled for today. They are even taking naps, especially the elders. It was a tiring ride for them here," Cavelan explained and then continued, "We didn't want to leave our parents alone at home. They enjoy coming here."

"I understand. It's always good to see them. We will have a delicious dinner later. If you or anyone needs anything at all, please let me know. Solinara will be checking in with you too. She will make some tea and have her wonderful desserts and cookies for you and your family whenever you need them."

"Thank you, Gateskin. I will let everyone know. The children will never refuse food, especially pastries of any kind, even though they already had some snacks."

"I have to check with my guards now, and will be back later. We can talk more then."

"That's fine. If you need me to assist in any way, you know where to find me," Cavelan replied.

Solinara was waiting to speak with Gateskin when he returned to the kitchen.

"Everything okay?"

"Yes, he understands that we will not bother the dragons for a visit today. We can go there tomorrow. I think the dragons need to rest and eat and nothing else. Also, Cavelan said his family was tired and need to rest too."

"Yes, I agree. It must have been frightening for the dragons to have this woman here. As for our visitors, that is a good idea to let them rest until tomorrow."

"Well, dragons don't get frightened easily. But I think Madrigal was quite wary about letting her near his children. In fact, he said he couldn't smell Elowen until after the dragonets stressed that she exuded a horrible and nauseating smell. I suspect that maybe Elowen knows about the dragonets and wanted to see them for herself."

"Really? How would she know about them, and if she knows, her parents must know too."

"I suspect so but we will know soon enough if King Marcellus and Queen Isla come for a visit."

"About the scent, did you smell it?"

"No, dragons have a much keener sense of smell that humans do."

"That is a good way to know if she comes back. They will smell her coming."

"Yes, I guess that will be our deterrent in keeping her at bay, Solinara. I always need your views about everything. I hadn't given that any thought yet."

"Do you want me to bring them their food? I have plenty of food made in the workshop. That is also something I wanted to discuss with you, Gateskin."

"What is that, Solinara?"

"The distribution of the food. It seems that this is all we do all day – deliver food to the dragons and other animals. Can't we come up with another way to do this. After all, we are a fairy and wizard with powers."

"Hmm, yes, I see what you mean, Solinara. I agree. What about if we give the Sprites the job of distributing the food to the dragons. The children will keep delivering the food to the wolves and barn animals. That is part of their chores anyway."

"I was thinking along the same lines too, Gateskin."

"How will the tiny Sprites deliver large bags of food to the dragons?"

"Well, I will put a spell over each bag enabling the Sprites to carry them. They will be a lot lighter in weight because of my spells. We will give them a timetable to follow. Abason, Head Counsel of the Sprites and Anabal, his wife, can decide who to give the jobs to each day. They can take turns. I think the Sprites will be excited to do this. Some of them would love to see the dragons up close."

"I think that will work! I like that idea. Good thinking, Solinara. I will have to explain all this to the dragons so that they don't frighten the Sprites when they begin delivering the food."

"Yes, most definitely. The dragons need to know that this will be a new way to receive their food. Also, we need to let the Sprites know they are safe and will not be harmed by the dragons," Solinara added.

"For now, I will bring it to the dragons until we get this schedule worked out. The children can deliver the food to the other animals. That will keep them busy. They appear to be antsy.

Maybe the visiting children would like to help them."

"Yes, I will tell them to do that. The other children will get a thrill out of helping them as long as Serena prepares the wolves for new people."

"Of course, dear. She will do what she needs to do to keep them safe and at a distance."

When Serena arrived at the wolves' hut, they were roaming around the borders and sniffing the areas when the children arrived there to feed them.

Serena stopped the others from getting too close when she spied large eyes looking back at her at the borders. She called out to her siblings to look. "Stay back!"

"What is that?" Simon asked as he backed away.

"I don't know. It could be some Catlings but the eyes are bigger and yellow."

"Will they be able to get inside the border?" Catalina asked, her voice quivering.

"No, I don't think so. Besides the wolves are there sniffing at the borders and know that something is there. They will not allow whatever it is to come through," Serena explained.

"Are those more wolves with the large yellow eyes?" Adolphin asked.

"I don't know for sure," Serena responded. "It's better if you all go back inside. I will have my father check this out. It may not be safe to stay here."

Anatonia Noella cried, "I don't like those eyes. They are scary. I'm going back inside. Come with me, Catalina."

Catalina nodded, turned and ran inside with Anatonia in the lead. Simon and Adolphin followed closely behind leaving Serena standing there to look at the menacing eyes that continued to look back at her.

She messaged her father who came out of the workshop with his hands full of food for the dragons.

"What's going on, Serena? Are you all right? Something wrong with the wolves?"

She pointed to the border where the eyes looked back at them.

"Looks like we have more visitors." Gateskin kept his voice calm so as not to frighten his daughter.

"What is that, Father? Could it be more Catlings that were deformed?"

"That is a possibility. Go back inside. I will check this out. Before you go, ask Cantok what he thinks it is."

Serena spoke in her mind to Cantok, leader of the wolves and waited to hear what he had to say.

"He says that it is a deformed Catling that was missed by the dragons. It is trying to come inside the border. He had to move his cubs inside the hut because it was trying to reach them."

"It's hungry and will not stop until it gets inside even if it gets zapped by the spell on the border. I need to put another spell on the border there. Go inside now and let your mother know what is going on. I will return shortly after dropping off this food for the dragons."

"Will the wolves be okay until then, Father?"

"Yes, they will keep the Catling from getting inside until I return. They will kill it before letting it harm their cubs."

"Okay. Please be careful, Father. I will tell Mother what is happening."

"Thank you, Serena. Don't worry. I will handle this."

He sent a message to the Head Guards to keep watch over the border with the wolves until he returned.

# CHAPTER FORTY-TWO

Spindle and Mitteran responded to the King's message about the errant Catling.

They flew over to the wolves' huts to keep watch over the eyes that looked back at them.

Gateskin dropped off the food and spoke with the dragons. "I may need your help destroying an errant Catling that is at the border around the wolves' hut. It is trying to get inside to snatch the cubs for a meal. It is definitely deformed by the looks of its huge eyes."

"Do you need me to come with you now?"

"Yes, after you have something to eat. I don't want you to be hungry."

"Being hungry may be a good thing, King. I can eat the Catling."

"Not a good idea, Madrigal. Remember they are deformed by a potion made by Queen Beregina of Parotovina. I cannot let you take a chance to become deformed too if you eat it."

"Okay, I will have something to eat later, if there is anything left. My offspring will probably eat it all before I get a chance anyway."

"You can get something to eat when we get back to the workshop, if that happens. The Queen has plenty of food there for another meal."

“That sounds good to me. Let’s go take care of this Catling. I’ll eat later.”

Solinara came out of the house to meet Gateskin. Serena had told her about the Catling at the border.

Gateskin explained what he and Madrigal were going to do. She hurried back inside to keep everyone away from the windows until it was all over.

Serena and her siblings kept the other children busy so that they didn’t see what Madrigal would have to do. They didn’t see the dragon flying there because they were in the play room at the back of the house. They did keep asking what would be done to the thing that was looking at them.

“No worries. My father is taking care of it. We can go outside later after it is safe once again,” Serena explained.

“What is he going to do?” Adolphin asked further.

"We will find out later. Don't worry. He can handle anything," Serena stressed.

Simon pulled out some of his soldiers and began to line them up to keep Adolphin occupied. He planned on moving them and flying them around the room.

Catalina shared what she could do with her dolls by making them disappear along with herself. This kept Anatonia so enthralled that she forgot all about the huge eyes that were looking back at her a short time ago.

Madrigal flew over the border where the errant Catling was lurking. He blew smoke over the animal that was deformed with a huge head, eyes and more legs than usual. Its tail had grown longer and swung back and forth trying to break down the border. Its extended claws reached inside and got zapped repeatedly as it tried to reach the wolves and their cubs.

Cantok, the leader of the wolves, scratched the Catling's paw as it tried to enter the border, deterring it from doing that again.

Madrigal kept blowing smoke over the creature and watched as it slowly fell asleep. He pulled it away from the border and further into the UT as he prepared to burn it until it was just ashes.

As he was doing this, another Catling came up to see what he was doing. It did not interfere for fear of being grabbed by the sharp claws of the enormous dragon.

This Catling was normal and appeared to be relieved that the deformed one was being destroyed by the dragon.

Madrigal blew out fire onto the sleeping Catling and kept this up until it was just ashes. The other Catling quickly turned around and ran away.

The dragon kept his eyes on the departing Catling as it raced away to ensure that it was not returning. Madrigal flew down beside the King and told him the job was finished.

"Thank you, Madrigal. Good job. I couldn't have done this without you."

"My pleasure, King Gateskin. I'm sure you would have come up with something to destroy it if I wasn't here."

"Maybe so, but I am happy that you are here, my friend."

Madrigal grinned and sighed contented until his stomach growled in discontent. "Sorry about that, King. Dragons are always hungry and need to eat many times a day."

"Come with me. Let's get some food for you after that successful demise of the Catling."

"Sounds good to me."

After Madrigal had eaten his fill, he mentioned the other Catling that was watching him as he destroyed the deformed creature.

King Gateskin asked, "Did it try to get close to you?"

"Oh no, it wouldn't have been that stupid to do that. It appeared to be curious about what I was doing and even looked relieved after it was done."

"Really? The deformed Catling must have been attacking the others for food."

# CHAPTER FORTY-THREE

In Parotovina a curious guard looked for the place where the fake medallion was buried earlier. He did not see any marker or where the ground was newly dug. He kept moving further into the woods. He was so intent on finding the burial site of the fake medallion that he didn't see the creatures that were now coming up behind him.

The Sprites in the trees sent out a warning cry to the guard. "Don't look behind you, stretch your arms up and we will help bring you out of the forest."

The guard ignored the Sprites' warning and looked behind him and cried out as he saw several strange-looking creatures looking back at him. They were black as night and had eyes that glowed. They stood on two legs and looked something like a bear only with long hair all over. Their arms and legs were part human including their heads. They reached out to the guard with claws on the end of their large hands.

The Sprites sent down sparks that they created by rubbing against the branches of the trees to try to deter the creatures away from the guard. The guard cowered and closed his eyes as the creatures moved closer to him.

The Sprites again sent sparks at the creatures and reached down to pull the man up into the trees where he huddled close to a large branch and shivered in fear.

The guard looked at the Sprites and said, "Why did you save me?"

"We will never harm anyone. We are not evil creatures like those below. We value life and always do good."

"I can't thank you enough. But how do I get back down now that I am stuck up here? I can't go that way since those creatures are still there."

"We will have to move you between the trees and get you close to the village and then you will be able to climb down to safety."

"What are those creatures? Where did they come from? I've never seen them before in the woods here."

"We don't know either. This is the first time we have spotted them. There are several roaming around below now. They appear to be looking for a way to get up here."

"You can't let them get me, please!" the guard begged.

"No, we won't let them. They could harm us and our families too."

"What are you going to do?"

"We will move you to another tree like we explained and keep moving you that way until you get to your village."

"Okay. I hope I can do this. I've never been up in a tree like this," the man remarked, in a shaky voice.

One Sprite sent word to Abason, leader of the Sprites, about the creatures and the guard. Abason contacted his son, Spindle to let him know of this impending danger.

"Is the guard safe, Father?"

"Yes, they are moving him from tree to tree until they get him into the village. We need to alert the villages all over the province about these creatures. They are large and appear to be half human and half animal like a bear."

"Oh, just what we need, another creature!" Spindle declared with a sigh. "I will let King Gateskin know."

"The guard, I'm sure, will share this news with his village and warn others not to go into the woods in Parotovina."

"I hope they heed the warning, Father. Keep your eyes on them until I can come there to see for myself."

"That is not necessary, son. It is too dangerous. Let King Gateskin handle things. He will have to inform the other rulers about this new danger."

"Yes, I'm sure he will do that right away. Stay safe, Father. Keep my fellow Sprites safe too."

"I always do, Spindle. That is my job to watch over all of you."

"Thank you, Father."

Spindle flew over to find King Gateskin to share this new impending danger.

Gateskin was looking over the borders behind the wolves' huts to ensure that no more errant Catlings were there when he looked up to see Spindle hovering over him.

"What's wrong, Spindle?"

"Sorry to bother you, King. It has been a grueling time lately and I hate to give you more unsavory news."

"Just tell me, Spindle. Yes, it has been a busy time recently in Sovorotskina but I'm ready for whatever it is you have to share."

"Okay." Spindle shared what he knew about these new creatures in the woods of Parotovina and waited to hear what the King planned to do.

"I see. More creatures for us to keep at bay. I need to alert the other rulers about this right away. There could be more out there. If the Kings do not have their borders safe then these creatures will get in and kill their villagers."

Spindle followed the King into his Conference room after Gateskin pulled Cavelan in along with him. They waited as Gateskin opened the Conference Spell to the other villages.

The first ruler that came into view was King Noderan of Amora which bordered Parotovina to the east followed by King Zuri of Merlina, next door neighbor to Parotovina, and finally The Healers of Merona, the village that was situated in the center of the province. The only ruler who did not appear, as usual, was King Kaposkaran of Parotovina, farther to the south.

The rulers looked at Gateskin and waited for an explanation why they were being summoned again.

"I have some disturbing news, Kings. Some Sprites in the woods around Parotovina reported that they rescued a guard from a bear-like creature. It was reported to be half human and half bear with long hair and sharp claws."

"What? In Parotovina?" King Noderan of Amora exclaimed.

"Yes, unfortunately. There were several reported wandering around in the woods. Evidently, they were looking for food per the Sprites who are monitoring them."

"But are they in other woods too?" King Zuri of Merlina asked, frowning and shaking his head.

"What can we do, Gateskin, to keep these creatures out of our villages?" The Healers of Merona, enquired.

"Does King Kaposkaran know about this danger? He isn't here." Noderan added.

"First of all, I do not know if there are any others around in your woods. As for keeping them out of your villages, I will explain. The answer to your last question is, Kaposkaran may already know about this because it was one of his guards that the Sprites rescued. I did send a call his way as I did to all of you. He doesn't always answer my calls. This time he will be sorry."

The rulers of Merlina and Amora were looking at each other and sighing. "What are we going to do if these creatures come into our woods and enter our villages?"

Gateskin responded in a firm voice, "You will need to ensure that your borders are protected with spells as you once did to keep the Catlings out. Have you checked them recently and reinforced them?"

"Umm…no…we didn't see any need to do that, Gateskin," the rulers of Merlina and Amora stressed.

"Well, now you will definitely need to do that. Have your wizards, or whoever is powerful enough, to do this right away. If you cannot do this, let me know. I will help you in whatever way I can."

Gateskin was already musing about how he would do this as the face of King Kaposkaran appeared looking disgruntled as usual.

When Kaposkaran saw the faces of the other rulers, he knew that something was terribly wrong. He suspected that it was the creature that almost got his guard in the woods.

# CHAPTER FORTY-FOUR

Gateskin closed all the windows of the Conference Call after finishing with the rulers. He and Cavelan discussed what they would have to do to protect Noella Province from this new peril.

"I think I will have to travel home and take care of my borders, Gateskin. I will return as soon as I can ensure they are safe, tight and nothing can enter."

"That is a good idea, Cavelan. We will discuss this more when you return. It may be better not to share this news with our families. We don't want to frighten them. Even so, we are not yet sure if these creatures have moved beyond the woods of Parotovina. It is better to be safe though."

"I agree. I will have to share something with my wife as you will with yours, I'm sure. Savina will not accept a lame excuse that I forgot something at home."

"I see what you mean, Cavelan. I will not get by without sharing this with Solinara either. She sees right through me."

"We will have to make sure that our children do not know anything about this. We don't want them to be frightened any more than they already are about these creatures that keep appearing."

"My children are not as resilient as yours are, Gateskin. Look how my two reacted when we were going to meet the dragons. They were already thinking that they were going to be eaten."

"That is understandable, Cavelan. They don't know anything about them. I assure you that they will love the dragons as much as my children do, once they meet them."

"I'm sure you are right, Gateskin. Well, I better speak with Savina and hurry home. I want to alert my guards to keep watch over the borders while we are away after I reinforce them."

Ever watchful, Spindle waited quietly for further instructions from the King after Gateskin and King Cavelan finished speaking. He could see that Gateskin was deeply disturbed.

"Spindle, stay here with me while I speak with my wife. She will have many questions and you can relate what your Sprites told you."

Solinara was in the kitchen as usual and heard her husband's voice calling her to come to the Conference Room right away.

Gateskin met her at the door and closed it to soundproof it. Solinara frowned when she saw the strain on her husband's face once again.

"What is wrong, dear?"

Gateskin sighed and began to share his latest concern. He asked Spindle to step in and explain in more detail.

"Oh my god! What are we going to do? How are we going to keep these creatures from moving through the woods and coming here?" Solinara exclaimed in shock.

Gateskin explained what he had told the rulers about reinforcing their borders.

"But they need to be eliminated, Gateskin!" Solinara stressed. "They could come here and …."

"No, Solinara, they will not come here. I will reinforce all the borders of our village once again. Besides, if they do try to come into the UT they will have to contend with the Catlings. It could be a bloody battle between them. Our wolves will patrol the border near our homes and alert me if they do see anything."

"Serena will have to explain all this to them," Solinara added.

"Yes, of course. They do listen to her. But I hesitate to share all this with her. It may frighten her. Though I know how strong she is."

"I think she can handle almost anything dear. She will have to keep this from her siblings and the other children."

"Yes, I agree, Solinara."

Spindle cleared his throat and spoke, "King, can we have the dragons go there and incinerate the creatures?"

"We may eventually have to do that if they keep multiplying."

"Do you think that Queen Beregina may have had something to do with these creatures?" Solinara asked.

"Hmm, I hadn't considered that, dear. You may be right about that. She is careless with her potions. She may have left one out and a bear somehow got it."

"That could explain why these creatures are so strange. Or maybe some men took the potion and changed."

"We will have to speak with King Kaposkaran and let him ask his wife about this possibility."

"He won't like it one bit," Solinara stated with a deep sigh.

"I'm well aware of that, Solinara." Gateskin frowned as he mused about what he would do next.

# CHAPTER FORTY-FIVE

Gateskin paid a visit to the dragons and informed them about the newest threat. He would have to ensure that the dragons were ready to do whatever he needed them to do to stop these creatures.

Madrigal came out after Gateskin called out to him. The dragon looked as if he had been napping.

"Did I disturb you, Madrigal?"

"Oh no, I was just taking a little snooze with my offspring. They are always tired from all the flying they do to hone their skills. Trying to keep them in order tires me out too."

"Hmm, I see, as long as you are wide awake for what I have to share with you now. Also, my children do not know anything about this. I want this to stay between us. You may share it with Izara but tell your dragonets that they need to keep quiet about it."

"I am now wide awake, King. Yes, I promise to keep this quiet. What is it about? Are there more Catlings that have to be destroyed?" Madrigal's eyes grew wide in anticipation.

"No, not Catlings, something else."

"Another creature?"

"Yes, unfortunately. This one is larger and could be formidable. We don't know what it is capable of yet."

"Is it bigger than me?" Madrigal asked, suddenly looking a little anxious.

"Not at all, Madrigal. Nothing is as large as you."

"That's good to hear. I always like to have the upper hand."

Gateskin described what had taken place in the woods of Parotovina and what the creatures looked like.

"That is quite strange, King. I never heard of such creatures. Part bear and part human, that is very weird."

"It is, Madrigal. That is why I need you to fly with me to check them out. I will have to put an Invisibility Spell over us in order to fly there under cover. I don't want to alarm any of the other villages if they see you. I don't think they are ready for that yet."

"Well, eventually they will have to see us."

"Yes, but not yet. They are all upset about these new creatures. I want to see the creatures for myself and try to figure out how dangerous they are and how strong they are too."

"Well, I can handle them, King. All I have to do is use smoke and then fire to end them once and for all."

"Yes, I realize that, Madrigal. What I need to do is figure out if they are more human than animal. If they are, maybe there will be a way to change them back to their human states as I did once before with the Quintaroons."

"How will you do that, King?" Madrigal asked, looking perplexed.

"Well, I need to find out before we leave if Queen Beregina had anything to do with these creatures."

"Do you think she used potions on them like she did with the Catlings?"

"She may have. I don't want to destroy humans if this is possible."

"I understand. When will you know if this is possible?"

"I am going to call King Kaposkaran again and find out before we leave."

"Do you want me to wait here, King?"

"Yes, I will be back shortly or at least as quickly as I can. You never know when or how long it will be before King Kaposkaran responds to my Conference Call."

Madrigal nodded and went back inside to share this new development with his mate. His dragonets were all ears and wanted to know everything too.

"You must not share this with the royal children. I promised the King that I would keep this between us."

"Okay, Father. Can we help in some way?" Lorcan asked with a wide grin.

"No, absolutely not! You *will* stay here under your mother's watchful wings and obey her every command. Do you hear me?"

Lorcan nodded and sighed.

"Yes, Father," Sunniva added and drew closer to hear every word.

After hearing about these creatures, the dragonets were flying up and down. "Are you sure we cannot help you destroy them, Father? Three who can shoot smoke and fire would be better than just one."

"Yes, Father. We have both been practicing shooting out smoke and fire and have become quite proficient," Sunniva exclaimed with a broad grin.

"No, Lorcan and Sunniva. You are not ready for this. Besides, I am not sure if the King wants me to destroy them yet. He wants to ensure first that they are not human."

"How can they be human if they look like a bear?" Sunniva asked.

"I don't know, sweet one. But I will soon find out."

In the meantime, King Gateskin was conversing with King Kaposkaran who surprisingly opened up his window to Gateskin's call right away.

"Ahh, good to see you Kaposkaran. Have you been working on your borders?"

"Yes, I have. My wife is helping me too. My guard told me about these new creatures. He was quite frightened by them and has since stayed in his home under my wife's care. She had to give him a potion to calm him down."

"Hmm, I see. Oh, there is something else I wanted to ask you. Do you think your wife had something to do with these creatures? They are half human and half bear. How could that happen unless there was a potion to do that?"

"Are you saying that you think my wife did this on purpose?"

"No, I think that it is possible some of the potion that she sent to capture my dragons may have gotten ingested by a human or a bear."

"I don't think she would be so careless. I…I…will have to speak with her. I don't promise anything though. She and I don't talk unless absolutely necessary since the last potion issue. I am fortunate that she is helping me secure the borders."

"I need to know about this right away. I have plans to destroy these creatures to keep our province safe. If they are human, then I cannot do that. Please ask her right away. I will wait here for your answer."

"Okay. I can't promise she will give me an answer though."

Gateskin waited several minutes which turned into a half an hour before Kaposkaran's face appeared again.

"She doesn't think she left out her potions where anything could have come in contact with them."

"Is she absolutely sure about that?"

"I had my guard search the area in and around her workshop. All appear to be neat and tidy and all potions are capped off and locked away."

"What about the remnants of the Catlings that you had buried. Any of the carcasses around for someone or something to eat?"

"No, I had my guards bury everything deep in the woods."

"In the woods?" Gateskin asked, as he shook his head in disbelief.

"Yes. Oh no!!" Kaposkaran's eyes grew wide as he said this.

***

Deep in the woods of Parotovina the creatures roamed freely looking for food. They were growing larger and stronger each day, existing on small animals and birds, or anything else that they could fit inside their mouths.

They would soon have to venture further into the areas beyond the woods to find larger prey.

Watch for Book 6 in this series coming later this year or next.

# ABOUT THE AUTHOR

Janice Spina is a retired administrative secretary from the Methuen Public School System in Massachusetts. She has always loved writing poetry, novels and children's stories. She published her first book in 2013 and hasn't stopped since.

This is the 51st book Janice has published. She also has two mystery series of six books each, one for boys and the other for girls which are enjoyed by both boys and girls. She has published 23 children's stories for young children. She writes under J.E. Spina, and has published nine novels and two short story collections for 18+.

She can be reached at these links.

Website: https://Jemsbooks.com
Blog: https://Jemsbooks.blog
Twitter: https://twitter.com/janice_spina

FB Main Page:
https://facebook.com/janice.spina.9
FB Author Page:
https://facebook.com/janicespina7
FB Novelist Page:
https://facebook.com/jespina7
Bluesky:
Https://www.bluesky.Janicespina.social.
Instagram:
Https://www.instagram.com/janicespina
LinkedIn: Https://LinkedIn.com/pub/Janice-spina
Goodreads:
Https://goodreads.com/user/show/17094469-Janice-spina
Amazon Author Page Children's and MG/PT/YA Books:
Https://Amazon.com/author/janicespina7
Amazon Author Page for Novels:
Https://Amazon.com/author/jespina77
Barnes & Noble: Janice Spina | Barnes & Noble®

Janice lives in New Hampshire with her husband, John, and a tank of tropical fish. John is the illustrator of her children's books and designer of all her book covers.

If you enjoyed this book, please leave a review where you purchased it and spread the word to your family and friends. Janice loves to hear from readers and welcomes reviews from wherever her books are purchased. She says, 'It's like Christmas each time I receive a review!'

If you would like to be on Janice Spina's email list to receive updates, newsletters, and special deals on books, please follow her blog at link above.

Watch for more books coming from JemsBooks.

# A NOTE FROM THE AUTHOR

Book 1 of this series was written many years ago. At that time, I wasn't ready to publish it. There were too many other books I wanted to publish first. I've always enjoyed reading fantasy and wanted to create my own fantasy series for young adults. This is Book 5 in the continuing saga of ***Gateskin Chronicles***.

This series is written for young adults - Ages 15+, but can be enjoyed by adults too. I consider this series to be PG-13 and up. It is up to parents to use their discretion about whether your younger children should read this series. Some things may not be suitable for them. There is never any vulgar language in any of my books but there are some situations that may be too violent for younger readers.

I hope you enjoyed this work of fiction. Watch for more books in this series coming over the next year or so.

Thank you for purchasing one of JemsBooks. I appreciate your kind support of me and my books. If you like this book, a review would be greatly appreciated wherever you purchased it. Reviews and word of mouth are the best way to spread your thoughts about books. Please share your review with friends and family. I would love to hear from you. You can reach me at jjspina@comcast.net.

All my books are available on Amazon and Barnes & Noble. Watch for more books coming for all ages.

With Blessings & Love,

Janice Spina

# YA BOOKS BY JANICE SPINA - PG 13+

***The Legend of the Taken Ones: Gateskin Chronicles Book 1***

Mom's Choice Awards - Gold Medal

Book Excellence Award Finalist

***The Unknown Territory: Gateskin Chronicles Book 2***

Mom's Choice Awards - Gold Medal

Maincrest Media Book Awards

*Search for the Medallion: Gateskin Chronicles Book 3*

Mom's Choice Awards - Gold Medal

*Return of the Dragons: Gateskin Chronicles Book 4*

Mom's Choice Awards - Gold Medal

**One more book coming!**

# OTHER MG/PT BOOKS BY JANICE SPINA - 10+

*Davey & Derek Junior Detectives Book 1:*
*The Case of the Missing Cell Phone*
Pinnacle Book Achievement Award
Honorable Mention- Readers' Favorite Book Award

*Davey & Derek Junior Detectives Book 2:*
*The Case of the Mysterious Black Cat*
Pinnacle Book Achievement Award

*Davey & Derek Junior Detectives Book 3: The Case of the Magical Ivory Elephant*
Pinnacle Book Achievement Award

Reader's Favorite Book Awards – Silver Medal

***Davey & Derek Junior Detectives Book 4: The Case of the Brown Scraggly Dog***
Top Shelf Book Awards – First Place
Finalist in Red City Review Awards
5-Star Book Review – Readers' Favorite Book Awards

***Davey & Derek Junior Detectives Book 5:***
***The Case of the Sad Mischievous Ghost***
Pinnacle Book Achievement Award
Authorsdb Cover Contest – Silver Medal

***Davey & Derek Junior Detectives Book 6: The Case of the Mystery of the Bells***
Pinnacle Book Achievement Award

Finalist – Readers' Favorite Book Awards
Finalist – Book Excellence Awards

*Abby & Holly School Dance*
Pinnacle Book Achievement Award
Bronze Medal from Readers' Favorite Book Awards

*Abby & Holly Series Book 2: Unfortunate Events*
Pinnacle Book Achievement Award
Readers' Favorite Book Awards – Honorable Mention

*Abby & Holly Series, Book 3, Secrets of the Trunk*
Pinnacle Book Achievement Award

*Abby & Holly Series, Book 4, The Hidden Stairway*

Pinnacle Book Achievement Award

*Abby & Holly Series, Book 5, The Copper Key*

Pinnacle Book Achievement Award

*Abby & Holly Series, Book 6, Faulty Timeline*

Pinnacle Book Achievement Award

**More MG/PT books coming over the next few years!**

# BOOKS BY J.E. SPINA FOR 15+

*The Misunderstood Angel (Branyrd the Angel Series Book 1)*

Five-Star review from Readers Favorite Book Awards

*Mission of Mercy (Branyrd the Angel Series Book 2)*

*Mission of Love (Branyrd the Angel Series Book 3)*

*Mission of Hope (Branyrd the Angel Series Book 4)*

# BOOKS BY J.E. SPINA FOR 18+

*Hunting Mariah*

Finalist in Authorsdb First Lines Contest

Maincrest Media Book Awards

*Mariah's Revenge*

Finalist in Authorsdb First Lines Contest

*How Far is Heaven*

Five-Star review from Readers' Favorite Book Awards

***An Angel Among Us: A Short Story Collection***

Five-Star review from Readers' Favorite Book Awards

***In A Second***

Five-Star review from Readers' Favorite Book Awards

***Lubelia Alycea: One Hundred Years***

Five-Star review from Readers' Favorite Book Awards

www.ingramcontent.com/pod-product-compliance
Lightning Source LLC
LaVergne TN
LVHW020517100826
845148LV00010B/1262

* 9 7 9 8 9 8 7 4 6 4 6 8 7 *